Cascades

Cascades consultants:
John Mannion, Head of English at Elliott School, Wandsworth
Sheena Davies, Head of English at Bishopbriggs High School,
Glasgow
Adrian Jackson, Advisory teacher for English
Geoff Fox, Lecturer at the University of Exeter School of
Education, and a National Curriculum Advisor

Spies I Have Known
and other stories

ABOUT THE AUTHOR

Doris Lessing was born in 1919 in Persia (now Iran). Her parents were both British, and she moved with them to Southern Rhodesia (now Zimbabwe) when she was five. She spent her childhood on a large farm there and first came to England in 1949, bringing with her the manuscript of her first novel, *The Grass in Singing*, which was published in 1950. It had outstanding success in Britain, America and ten European countries.

Since then her international reputation not only as a novelist, but as a non-fiction and short-story writer has flourished, and she has won numerous prizes.

Other titles in the *Cascades* series which you might enjoy are:

It's My Life   ROBERT LEESON

A realistic and moving novel which examines the complex emotions experienced by Jan when her mother walks out on the family, and she is left to run the home. She finds herself unable to conform to the expectations of relatives and friends and resolves to run her life her own way. With this increased self-awareness comes a clearer understanding of the reason why her mother left.

Somehow Tenderness Survives   SELECTED BY HAZEL ROCHMAN

This is a collection of ten short stories by South African writers such as Nadine Gordimer, Mark Mathabane and Doris Lessing. The stories create a moving and sometimes shockingly vivid portrait of how apartheid affects every young South African.

The Owl Service   ALAN GARNER

In a big house in a Welsh valley, Roger and Alison, a young English step-brother and sister, live uneasily with Gwyn, the housekeeper. There's a power stirring in the valley that dates from a sad and distant myth, forcing them, like many in their place before, into a vicious predicament that looks likely to end up in violent disaster.

Words By Heart   OUIDA SEBESTYEN

Had Lena overstepped her bounds by winning the contest that every one thought the white boy would win? This book tells a universal story of the risk of reaching out, to grasp and affirm life.

DORIS LESSING

Spies
I Have
Known
and other stories

'Through the Tunnel' © Doris Lessing 1954
'Pleasure', 'Flight' © Doris Lessing 1957
First published in Great Britain by MacGibbon and Kee Ltd 1957
Published by Granada Publishing 1966
Published by Grafton Books 1985

'England Versus England', 'To Room 19', 'Notes for a Case History',
'How I Finally Lost My Heart' © Doris Lessing 1963
First published in Great Britain by MacGibbon and Kee Ltd 1963
Published by Grafton Books 1965
Published by Paladin 1992

'An Old Woman and Her Cat', 'Spies I Have Known', 'The Story of a,
Non-Marrying Man' © The Doris Lessing Trust 1972
First published in Great Britain by Jonathan Cape 1972
Published by Paladin Books 1990

ISBN 0 00 330309 8

This collection first published in *Cascades* in 1995 by Collins Educational

Printed in Great Britain by HarperCollins Manufacturing, Glasgow

Cover illustration: detail from *Interior with Japanese Fan*, c.1915, by
Samuel John Peploe (1871–1935) University of Hull Art Collection/
Bridgeman Art Library, London

THROUGH THE TUNNEL

Going to the shore on the first morning of the holiday, the young English boy stopped at a turning of the path and looked down at a wild and rocky bay, and then over to the crowded beach he knew so well from other years. His mother walked on in front of him, carrying a bright striped bag in one hand. Her other arm, swinging loose, was very white in the sun. The boy watched that white, naked arm, and turned his eyes, which had a frown behind them, towards the bay and back again to his mother. When she felt he was not with her, she swung around. 'Oh there you are, Jerry!' she said. She looked impatient, then smiled. 'Why, darling, would you rather not come with me? Would you rather—' She frowned, conscientiously worrying over what amusements he might secretly be longing for which she had been too busy or too careless to imagine. He was very familiar with that anxious, apologetic smile. Contrition sent him running after her. And yet, as he ran, he looked back over his shoulder at the wild bay; and all morning, as he played on the safe beach, he was thinking of it.

Next morning, when it was time for the routine of swimming and sunbathing, his mother said, 'Are you tired of the usual beach, Jerry? Would you like to go somewhere else?'

'Oh, no!' he said quickly, smiling at her out of that unfailing impulse of contrition - a sort of chivalry. Yet, walking down the path with her, he blurted out, 'I'd like to go and have a look at those rocks down there.'

She gave the idea her attention. It was a wild-looking place, and there was no one there, but she said, 'Of course, Jerry. When you've had enough, come to the big beach. Or just go straight back to the villa, if you like.' She walked away, that bare arm, now slightly reddened from yesterday's sun, swinging. And he almost ran after her again, feeling it unbearable that she should go by herself, but he did not.

She was thinking, Of course he's old enough to be safe without me. Have I been keeping him too close? He mustn't feel he ought to be with me. I must be careful.

He was an only child, eleven years old. She was a widow. She was determined to be neither possessive nor lacking in devotion. She went worrying off to her beach.

As for Jerry, once he saw that his mother had gained her beach, he began the steep descent to the bay. From where he was, high up among red-brown rocks, it was a scoop of moving bluish green fringed with white. As he went lower, he saw that it spread among small promontories and inlets of rough, sharp rock, and the crisping, lapping surface showed stains of purple and darker blue. Finally, as he ran sliding and scrapping down the last few yards, he saw an edge of white surf, and the shallow, luminous movement of water over white sand, and, beyond that, a solid, heavy blue.

He ran straight into the water and began swimming.

He was a good swimmer. He went out fast over the gleaming sand, over a middle region where rocks lay like discoloured monsters under the surface, and then he was in the real sea – a warm sea where irregular cold currents from the deep water shocked his limbs.

When he was so far out that he could look back not only on the little bay but past the promontory that was between it and the big beach, he floated on the buoyant surface and looked for his mother. There she was, a speck of yellow under an umbrella that looked like a slice of orange peel. He swam back to shore, relieved at being sure she was there, but all at once very lonely.

On the edge of a small cape that marked the side of the bay away from the promontory was a loose scatter of rocks. Above them, some boys were stripping off their clothes. They came running, naked, down to the rocks. The English boy swam towards them, and kept his distance at a stone's throw. They were of that coast, all of them burned smooth dark brown, and speaking a language he did not understand. To be with them, of them, was a craving that filled his whole body. He swam a little closer; they turned and watched him with narrowed, alert dark eyes. Then one smiled and waved. It was enough. In a minute, he had swum in and was on the rocks beside them, smiling with a desperate, nervous supplication. They shouted cheerful greetings at him, and then, as he preserved his nervous, uncomprehending smile, they understood that he was a foreigner strayed from his own beach, and they proceeded to forget him. But he was happy. He was with them.

They began diving again and again from a high point into a well of blue sea between rough, pointed rocks. After they had dived and come up, they swam around, hauled themselves up, and waited their turn to dive again. They were big boys – men to Jerry. He dived, and they watched him, and when he swam around to take his place, they made way for him. He felt he was accepted, and he dived again, carefully, proud of himself.

Soon the biggest of the boys poised himself, shot down into the water, and did not come up. The others stood about, watching. Jerry, after waiting for the sleek brown head to appear, let out a yell of warning; they looked at him idly and turned their eyes back towards the water. After a long time, the boy came up on the other side of a big dark rock, letting the air out of his lungs in a sputtering gasp and a shout of triumph. Immediately, the rest of them dived in. One moment, the morning seemed full of chattering boys; the next, the air and the surface of the water were empty. But through the heavy blue, dark shapes could be seen moving and groping.

Jerry dived, shot past the school of underwater swimmers, saw a black wall of rock looming at him, touched it, and bobbed up at once to the surface, where the wall was a low barrier he could see across. There was no one visible; under him, in the water, the dim shapes of the swimmers had disappeared. Then one, and then another of the boys came up on the far side of the barrier of rock, and he understood that they had swum through some gap or hole in it. He plunged down again. He could see nothing through the stinging salt water but the blank rock. When he came up, the boys were all on the diving rock, preparing to attempt the feat again. And now, in a panic of failure, he yelled up, in English, 'Look at me! Look!' and he began splashing and kicking in the water like a foolish dog.

They looked down gravely, frowning. He knew the

frown. At moments of failure, when he clowned to claim his mother's attention, it was with just this grave, embarrassed inspection that she rewarded him. Through his hot shame, feeling the pleading grin on his face like a scar that he could never remove, he looked up at the group of big brown boys on the rock and shouted, '*Bonjour! Merci! Au revoir! Monsieur, monsieur!*' while he hooked his fingers round his ears and waggled them.

Water surged into his mouth; he choked, sank, came up. The rock, lately weighed with boys, seemed to rear up out of the water as their weight was removed. They were flying down past him, now, into the water; the air was full of falling bodies. Then the rock was empty in the hot sunlight. He counted one, two, three . . .

At fifty, he was terrified. They must all be drowning beneath him, in the watery caves of the rock! At a hundred, he stared around him at the empty hillside, wondering if he should yell for help. He counted faster, faster, to hurry them up, to bring them to the surface quickly, to drown them quickly – anything rather than the terror of counting on and on into the blue emptiness of the morning. And then, at a hundred and sixty, the water beyond the rock was full of boys blowing like brown whales. They swam back to the shore without a look at him.

He climbed back to the diving rock and sat down, feeling the hot roughness of it under his thighs. The boys were gathering up their bits of clothing and running off along the shore to another promontory. They were leaving to get away from him. He cried openly, fists in his eyes. There was no one to see him, and he cried himself out.

It seemed to him that a long time had passed, and

he swam out to where he could see his mother. Yes, she was still there, a yellow spot under an orange umbrella. He swam back to the big rock, climbed up, and dived into the blue pool among the fanged and angry boulders. Down he went, until he touched the wall of rock again. But the salt was so painful in his eyes that he could not see.

He came to the surface, swam to shore and went back to the villa to wait for his mother. Soon she walked slowly up the path, swinging her striped bag, the flushed, naked arm dangling beside her. 'I want some swimming goggles,' he panted, defiant and beseeching.

She gave him a patient, inquisitive look as she said casually, 'Well, of course, darling.'

But now, now, now! He must have them this minute, and no other time. He nagged and pestered until she went with him to a shop. As soon as she had bought the goggles, he grabbed them from her hand as if she were going to claim them for herself, and was off, running down the steep path to the bay.

Jerry swam out to the big barrier rock, adjusted the goggles, and dived. The impact of the water broke the rubber-enclosed vacuum, and the goggles came loose. He understood that he must swim down to the base of the rock from the surface of the water. He fixed the goggles tight and firm, filled his lungs, and floated, face down, on the water. Now he could see. It was as if he had eyes of a different kind - fish-eyes that showed everything clear and delicate and wavering in the bright water.

Under him, six or seven feet down, was a floor of perfectly clean, shining white sand, rippled firm and hard by the tides. Two greyish shapes steered there, like long, rounded pieces of wood or slate. They were fish. He saw them nose towards each other, poise motionless, make a dart forward, swerve off, and come around again. It was like a water dance. A few inches above them the water sparkled as if sequins were dropping through it. Fish again – myriads of minute fish, the length of his fingernail, were drifting through the water, and in a moment he could feel the innumerable tiny touches of them against his limbs. It was like swimming in flaked silver. The great rock the big boys had swum through rose sheer out of the white sand, black, tufted lightly with greenish weed. He could see no gap in it. He swam down to its base.

Again and again he rose, took a big chestful of air, and went down. Again and again he groped over the surface of the rock, feeling it, almost hugging it in the desperate need to find the entrance. And then, once, while he was clinging to the black walls, his knees came up and he shot his feet out forward and they met no obstacle. He had found the hole.

He gained the surface, clambered about the stones that littered the barrier rock until he found a big one, and, with this in his arms, let himself down over the side of the rock. He dropped, with the weight, straight to the sandy floor. Clinging tight to the anchor of stone, he lay on his side and looked in under the dark shelf at the place where his feet had gone. He could see the hole. It was an irregular, dark gap, but he could not see deep into it. He let go of his anchor, clung with his hands to the edge of the hole, and tried to push himself in.

He got his head in, found his shoulders jammed, moved them in sidewise, and was inside as far as his waist. He could see nothing ahead. Something soft and clammy touched his mouth, he saw a dark frond moving

7

against the greyish rock, and panic filled him. He thought of octopuses, of clinging weed. He pushed himself backward and caught a glimpse, as he retreated, of a harmless tentacle of seaweed drifting in the mouth of the tunnel. But it was enough. He reached the sunlight, swam to shore, and lay on the diving rock. He looked down into the blue well of water. He knew he must find his way through that cave, or hole, or tunnel, and out the other side.

First, he thought, he must learn to control his breathing. He let himself down into the water with another big stone in his arms, so that he could lie effortlessly on the bottom of the sea. He counted. One, two, three. He counted steadily. He could hear the movement of blood in his chest. Fifty-one, fifty two . . . His chest was hurting. He let go of the rock and went up into the air. He saw that the sun was low. He rushed to the villa and found his mother at her supper. She said only, 'Did you enjoy yourself?' and he said, 'Yes.'

All night, the boy dreamed of the water-filled cave in the rock, and as soon as breakfast was over he went to the bay.

That night, his nose bled badly. For hours he had been underwater, learning to hold his breath, and now he felt weak and dizzy. His mother said, 'I shouldn't overdo things, darling, if I were you.'

That day and the next, Jerry exercised his lungs as if everything, the whole of his life, all that he would become, depended upon it. And again his nose bled at night, and his mother insisted on his coming with her the next day. It was a torment to him to waste a day of his careful self-training, but he stayed with her at that other beach, which now seemed a place for small children, a place where his mother might lie safe in the sun. It was not his beach.

He did not ask for permission, on the following day, to go to his beach. He went, before his mother could consider the complicated rights and wrongs of the matter. A day's rest, he discovered had improved his count by ten. The big boys had made the passage while he counted a hundred and sixty. He had been counting fast, in his fright. Probably now, if he tried, he could get through that long tunnel, but he was not going to try yet. A curious, most unchildlike persistence, a controlled impatience, made him wait. In the meantime, he lay underwater on the white sand, littered now by stones he had brought down from the upper air, and studied the entrance to the tunnel. He knew every jut and corner of it, as far as it was possible to see. It was as if he already felt its sharpness about his shoulders.

He sat by the clock in the villa, when his mother was not near, and checked his time. He was incredulous and then proud to find he could hold his breath without strain for two minutes. The words 'two minutes', authorized by the clock, brought the adventure that was so necessary to him close.

In another four days, his mother said casually one morning they must go home. On the day before they left, he would do it. He would do it if it killed him, he said defiantly to himself. But two days before they were to leave – a day of triumph when he increased his count by fifteen – his nose bled so badly that he turned dizzy and had to lie limply over the big rock like a bit of seaweed, watching the thick red blood flow on to the rock and trickle slowly down to the sea. He was frightened. Supposing he turned dizzy in the tunnel? Supposing he died there, trapped? Supposing – his head went

9

around, in the hot sun, and he almost gave up. He thought he would return to the house and lie down, and next summer, perhaps, when he had another year's growth in him – *then* he would go through the hole.

But even after he had made the decision, or thought he had, he found himself sitting up on the rock and looking down into the water, and he knew that now, this moment, when his nose had only just stopped bleeding, when his head was still sore and throbbing – this was the moment when he would try. If he did not do it now, he never would. He was trembling with fear that he would not go, and he was trembling with horror at that long, long tunnel under the rock, under the sea. Even in the open sunlight, the barrier rock seemed very wide and very heavy; tons of rock pressed down on where he would go. If he died there, he would lie until one day – perhaps not before next year – those big boys would swim into it and find it blocked.

He put on his goggles, fitted them tight, tested the vacuum. His hands were shaking. Then he chose the biggest stone he could carry and slipped over the edge of the rock until half of him was in the cool, enclosing water and half in the hot sun. He looked up once at the empty sky, filled his lungs once, twice, and then sank fast to the bottom with the stone. He let it go and began to count. He took the edges of the hole in his hands and drew himself into it, wriggling his shoulders in sidewise as he remembered he must, kicking himself along with his feet.

Soon he was clear inside. He was in a small rock-bound hole filled with yellowish-grey water. The water was pushing him up against the roof. The roof was sharp and pained his back. He pulled himself along with his hands – fast, fast – and used his legs as levers.

His head knocked against something; a sharp pain dizzied him. Fifty, fifty-one, fifty-two . . . He was without light, and the water seemed to press upon him with the weight of rock. Seventy-one, seventy-two . . . There was no strain on his lungs. He felt like an inflated balloon, his lungs were so light and easy, but his head was pulsing.

He was being continually pressed against the sharp roof, which felt slimy as well as sharp. Again he thought of octopuses, and wondered if the tunnel might be filled with weed that could tangle him. He gave himself a panicky, convulsive kick forward, ducked his head, and swam. His feet and hands moved freely, as if in open water. The hole must have widened out. He thought he must be swimming fast, and he was frightened of banging his head if the tunnel narrowed.

A hundred, a hundred and one . . . The water paled. Victory filled him. His lungs were beginning to hurt. A few more strokes and he would be out. He was counting wildly; he said a hundred and fifteen, and then, a long time later, a hundred and fifteen again. The water was a clear jewel-green all around him. Then he saw, above his head, a crack running up through the rock. Sunlight was falling through it, showing the clean dark rock of the tunnel, a single mussel shell, and darkness ahead.

He was at the end of what he could do. He looked up at the crack as if it were filled with air and not water, as if he could put his mouth to it to draw in air. A hundred and fifteen, he heard himself say inside his head – but he had said that long ago. He must go on into the blackness ahead, or he would drown. His head was swelling, his lungs cracking. A hundred and fifteen, a hundred and fifteen pounded through his head, and he feebly clutched at rocks in the dark, pulling himself forward, leaving the brief space of sunlit water behind. He felt he was dying. He was no longer quite conscious. He struggled on in the darkness between lapses into unconsciousness. An immense, swelling pain filled his head, and then the darkness cracked with an explosion of green light. His hands, groping forward, met nothing, and his feet, kicking back, propelled him out into the open sea.

He drifted to the surface, his face turned up to the air. He was gasping like a fish. He felt he would sink now and drown; he could not swim the few feet back to the rock. Then he was clutching it and pulling himself up on to it. He lay face down, gasping. He could see nothing but a red-veined, clotted dark. His eyes must have burst, he thought, they were full of blood. He tore off his goggles and a gout of blood went into the sea. His nose was bleeding, and the blood had filled the goggles.

He scooped up handfuls of water from the cool, salty sea, to splash on his face, and did not know whether it was blood or salt water he tasted. After a time, his heart quieted, his eyes cleared, and he sat up. He could see the local boys diving and playing half a mile away. He did not want them. He wanted nothing but to get back home and lie down.

In a short while, Jerry swam to shore and climbed slowly up the path to the villa. He flung himself on the bed and slept, waking at the sound of feet on the path outside. His mother was coming back. He rushed to the bathroom, thinking she must not see his face with bloodstains, or tearstains, on it. He came out of the bathroom and met her as she walked into the villa, smiling, her eyes lighting up.

'Have a nice morning?' she asked, laying her hand on his warm brown shoulder a moment.

'Oh, yes, thank you,' he said.

'You look a bit pale.' And then, sharp and anxious, 'How did you bang your head?'

'Oh, just banged it,' he told her.

She looked at him closely. He was strained. His eyes were glazed-looking. She was worried. And then she said to herself, Oh, don't fuss! Nothing can happen. He can swim like a fish.

They sat down to lunch together.

'Mummy,' he said, 'I can stay under water for two minutes – three minutes, at least.' It came bursting out of him.

'Can you, darling,' she said. 'Well, I shouldn't overdo it. I don't think you ought to swim any more today.'

She was ready for a battle of wits, but he gave in at once. It was no longer of the least importance to go to the bay.

PLEASURE

There were two great feasts, or turning-points, in Mary Rogers' year. She began preparing for the second as soon as the Christmas decorations were down. This year, she was leafing through a fashion magazine, when her husband said: 'Dreaming of the sun, old girl!'

'I don't see why not,' she said, rather injured. 'After all, it's been four years.'

'I really don't see how we can afford it.'

On her face he saw a look which he recognized.

Her friend Mrs Baxter, the manager's wife, also saw the magazine, and said: 'You'll be off to the south of France again, this year, I suppose. Now that your daughter won't be needing you.' She added those words which in themselves were justification for everything: 'We'll stay faithful to Brighton, I expect.'

And Mary Rogers said, as she always did: 'I can't imagine why anyone takes a holiday in Britain when the same money'd take them to the continent.'

For four years she had gone with her daughter and the grandchildren to Cornwall. It sounded a sacrifice on the altar of the family, the way she put it to her friends. But this year the daughter was going to the other grandmother in Scotland, and everyone knew it.

Everyone. That is, Mrs Baxter, Mrs Justin-Smith, and Mrs Jones.

Mary Rogers bought gay cottons and spread them over the living-room. Outside, a particularly grim February held the little Midlands town in a steady shiver. Rain swept the window panes. Tommy Rogers saw the cottons, and said not a word. But a week later she was fitting a white linen sun-suit before the mirror when he said: 'I say, old girl, that shows quite a big of leg, you know . . .'

At that moment it was acknowledged that they should go. Also, that the four years had made a difference in various ways. Mary Rogers secretly examined her thighs and shoulders before the glass, and thought they might very well be exposed. But the clothes she made were of the sensible but smart variety. She sewed at them steadily through the evenings of March, April, May, June. She was a good needlewoman. Also, for a few happy months before she married, she had studied fashion designing in London. That had been a different world. In speaking of it now, to the women of her circle – Mrs Baxter, Mrs Justin-Smith and Mrs Jones, her voice conveyed the degree of difference. And Mrs Baxter would say, kindly as always: 'Ah well, we none of us know what's in store for us when we're young.'

They were to leave towards the end of July. A week before, Tommy Rogers produced a piece of paper on which were set out certain figures. They were much lower figures than ever before. 'Oh, we'll manage,' said Mary vaguely. Her mind was already moving among scenes of blue sea, blue sky.

'Perhaps we'd better book at the Plaza.'

'Oh, surely no need. They know us there.'

The evening before they left, there was a bridge party in the Baxters' house for the jaunting couple. Tommy Rogers was seen to give his wife an uneasy glance as she said: 'With air travel as cheap as it is now, I really can't understand why . . .'

For they had booked by train, of course, as usual.

They successfully negotiated the Channel, a night in a Paris hotel, and the catching of the correct train.

In a few hours they would see the little village on the sea where they had first come twenty-five years ago on their honeymoon. They had chosen it because Mary Hill had met, in those artistic circles which she had enjoyed for alas so short a time, a certain well-known stage decorator who had a villa there. During that month of honeymoon, they had spent a happy afternoon at the villa.

As the train approached, she was looking to see the villa, alone on its hill above the sea. But the hill was now thick with little white villas, green-shuttered, red-roofed in the warm southern green.

'The place seems to have grown quite a bit,' said Tommy. The station had grown too. There was a long platform now, and a proper station building. And gazing down towards the sea, they saw a cluster of shops and casinos and cafés. Even four years before, there had been a single shop, a restaurant and a couple of hotels.

'Well,' said Mary bitterly, 'if the place is full of tourists now, it won't be the same at all.'

But the sun was shining, the sea tossed and sparkled, the palm trees stood along the white beach. They carried their suitcases down the slope of the road to the Plaza, feeling at home.

Outside the Plaza, they looked at each other. What

had been a modest building, was an imposing one, surrounded by gay awnings and striped umbrellas. 'Old Jacques is spreading himself,' said Tommy, and they walked up the neat gravel path to the foyer looking for Jacques, who had welcomed them so often.

At the office, Mary enquired in her stiff correct French for Monsieur Jacques. The clerk smiled and regretted that Monsieur Jacques had left them three years before. 'He knew us well,' said Mary, her voice coming aggrieved and shrill. 'He always had room for us here.'

But certainly there was a room for Madame. Most certainly. At once attendants came hurrying for the suitcases.

'Hold your horses a minute,' said Tommy. 'Wait. Ask what it costs now.'

Mary enquired, casually enough, what the rates now were. She received the information with a lengthening of her heavy jaw, and rapidly transmitted it to Tommy. He glanced, embarrassed, at the clerk, who, recognizing a situation, turned tactfully to a ledger and prepared to occupy himself so that the elderly English couple could confer.

'We can't, Mary. It's no good. We'd have to go back at the end of a week.'

'But we've always stayed here . . .'

At last she turned towards the clerk, who was immediately attentive, and said with a stiff smile: 'I'm afraid the currency regulations make things difficult for us.' She had spoken in English, such was her upset, and it was in English that he replied pleasantly: 'I understand perfectly, Madame. Perhaps you would care to try the Belle Vue across the street. There are many English people there.'

The Rogers left, carrying their two suitcases ignom-iniously down the neat gravelled path, among the gay tables where people already sat at dinner. The sun had gone down. Opposite, the Belle Vue was a glow of lights. Tommy Rogers was not surprised when Mary walked past it without a look. For years, staying at the Plaza, they had felt superior to the Belle Vue. Also, had that clerk not said it was full of English people?

Since this was France, and the season, the Agency was of course open. An attractive mademoiselle deplored that they had not booked rooms earlier.

'We've been here every year for twenty-five years,' said Mary, pardonably overlooking the last four, and another stretch of five when the child had been small. 'We've never had to book before.'

Alas, alas, suggested the mademoiselle with her shoulders and her pretty eyes, what a pity that St Nicole had become so popular, so attractive. There was no fact she regretted more. She suggested the Belle Vue.

The Rogers walked the hundred yards back to the Belle Vue, feeling they were making a final concession to fate, only to find it fully booked up. Returning to the Agency, they were informed that there was, hap-pily, one room vacant in a villa on the hillside. They were escorted to it. And now it was the turn of the pretty mademoiselle to occupy herself, not with a ledger, but in examining the view of brilliant stars and the riding-lights of ships across the bay, while the Rogers conferred. Their voices were now not only angry, but high with exasperation. For this room, an extremely small one, at the bottom of a big villa, stone-floored, uncarpeted, with a single large bed of the sort Mary always thought of as *French*, a wardrobe that was no wardrobe, since it had been filled with shelves, a sink, and a small gas stove, they were asked to pay a sum which filled them with disbelief. If they desired hot water, as the English so often do, they would have to heat it in a saucepan on the stove.

But, as the mademoiselle pointed out, turning from her appreciative examination of the exotic night scene, it would be such an advantage to do one's own cooking.

'I suggest we go back to the Plaza. Better one week of comfort than three of this,' said Mary. They returned to the Plaza to find that the room had been taken, and none were available.

It was now nearly ten in the evening, and the infinitely obliging mademoiselle returned them to the little room in the villa, for which they agreed to pay more than they had done four years before for comfort, good food, and hot water in the Plaza. Also, they had to pay a deposit of over ten pounds in case they might escape in the night with the bed, the wardrobe, or the tin spoons; or refused to pay the bills for electricity, gas, and water.

The Rogers went to bed immediately, worn out with travelling and disappointment.

In the morning, Mary announced that she had no intention of cooking on a holiday, and they took *petit-déjeuner* at a café, paid the equivalent of twelve shillings for two small cups of coffee and two rolls, and changed their minds. They would have to cook in the room.

Preserving their good humour with an effort, they bought cold food for lunch, left it in the room, and prepared themselves for enjoyment. For the sea was blue, blue and sparkling. And the sunshine was hot and golden. And after all, this was the South of France, the prettiest place in Europe, as they had always agreed.

And in England now, said the *Daily Telegraph*, it was pouring with rain.

On the beach was another bad moment. Umbrellas stretched six deep, edge to edge, for half a mile along the silvery beach. Bodies lay stretched out baking in the sun, hundreds to the acre, a perfect bed of heated brown flesh.

'They've ruined the place, ruined it,' cried Mary, as she surveyed the untidy scene. But she stepped heavily down into the sand, and unbuttoned her dress. She was revealed to be wearing a heavy black bathing costume; and she did not miss the relieved glance her husband gave her. She felt it to be unfair. There he stood, a tall, very thin, fair man, quite presentable in an absurd bathing slip, which consisted of six inches of material held on by a string round his hips. And there *she* was, a heavy firm woman, with clear white flesh – but middle-aged, and in a black bathing costume.

She looked about. Two feet away was a mess of tangled brown limbs belonging to half a dozen boys and girls, the girls wearing nothing but coloured cotton brassières and panties. She saw Tommy looking at them too. Then she noticed, eighteen inches to the other side, a vast grey-haired lady, bulging weary pallid flesh out of a white cotton play-suit. Mary gave her a look of happy superiority, and lay down flat on the sand, congratulating herself.

All the morning the English couple lay there, turning over and over on the sand like a pair of grilling herrings, for they felt their pale skins to be a shame and a disgrace. When they returned to their room for lunch, it was to find that swarms of small black ants had infested their cold meats. They were unable to mind very much, as it had become evident they had overdone the sunbathing. Both were bright scarlet, and their eyes ached. They lay down in the cool of the darkened room, feeling foolish to be such amateurs – they, who should know better! They kept their beds that afternoon, and the next day . . . several days passed. Sometimes, when hunger overcame them, Mary winced down to the village to buy cold food – impossible to keep supplies in the room because of the ants. After eating, she hastily washed up in the sink where they also washed. Twice a day, Tommy went reluctantly outside, while she washed herself inch by inch in water heated in the saucepan. Then she went outside while he did the same. After these indispensable measures of hygiene, they retired to the much too narrow bed, shrinking away from any chance of contact with each other.

At last the discomfort of the room, as much as their healing flesh, drove them forth again, more cautiously clothed, to the beach. Skin was ripping off them both in long shreds. At the end of a week, however, they had become brown and shining, able to take their places without shame among the other brown and glistening bodies that littered the beach like so many stranded fish.

Day after day the Rogers descended the steep path to the beach, after having eaten a hearty English breakfast of ham and eggs, and stayed there all morning. All morning they lay, and then all afternoon, but at a good distance from a colony of English which kept itself to itself some hundreds of yards away.

They watched the children screaming and laughing in the unvarying blue waves. They watched the groups of French adolescents flirt and roll each other over on the sand in a way which Mary, at least, thought appallingly free. Thank heavens her daughter had married young and was safely out of harm's way! Nothing could have persuaded Mary Rogers of the extreme respectability of these youngsters. She suspected them all of shocking and complicated vices. Incredible that in so few a number of years, they would be sorted by some powerful and comforting social process into these decent, well-fed French couples, each so anxiously absorbed in the welfare of one, or perhaps two small children.

They watched also, with admiration, the more hardened swimmers cleave out through the small waves into the sea beyond the breakwater with their masks, their airtubes, their frogs' feet.

They were content.

This is what they had come for. This is what all these hundreds of thousands of people along the coast had come for, to lie on the sand, and receive the sun on their heating bodies, to receive, too, in small doses, the hot blue water which dried too stickily on them. The sea was very salty, and warm-smelling – smelling of a little more than salt and weed, for beyond the breakwater the town's sewers spilled into the sea, washing back into the inner bay rich deposits which dried on the perfumed oiled bodies of the happy bathers.

This is what they had come for.

Yet, there was no doubt that in the Plaza things had been quite different. There, one rose late, lingered over coffee and rolls, descended, or did not descend, to the beach for a couple of hours' sun worship, returned to a lengthy lunch, slept, bathed again, enjoyed an even more lengthy dinner. That, too, was called a seaside holiday. Now, the beach was really the only place to go. From nine until one, from two until seven, the

Rogers were on it. It was a sea-holiday with a vengeance.

About the tenth day, they realized that half of their time had gone; and Tommy showed his restlessness, his feeling that there should be more to it than this, by diving into one of the new and so terribly expensive shops, and emerging with a mask, frogs' feet, and airtube. With an apology to Mary for leaving her, he plunged out into the bay, looking like – or so she rather tartly remarked – a space-man in a children's comic. He did not return for some hours.

'This is better than anything, old girl, you should try it,' he said, wading out of the sea with an absorbed excited look. That afternoon she spent on the beach alone, straining her eyes to make out which of the bobbing periscopes in the water was his.

Thus engaged, she heard herself addressed in English: 'I always say I am an undersea widow too.' She turned to see a slight girl, clearly English, with pretty fair curls, a neat blue bathing costume, pretty blue eyes, jolly legs stretched out in the warm sand. An English girl. But her voice was, so Mary decided, passable, in spite of a rather irritating giggle. She relented, and though it was her principle that one did not go to France to consort with the English, said: 'Is your husband out there?'

'Oh, I never see him between meals,' said the girl cheerfully, and lay back on the sand.

Mary thought that this girl was very similar to herself at that age – only, of course, *she* had known how to make the best of herself. They talked, in voices drugged by sea and sun, until first Tommy Rogers, and then the girl's husband, rose out of the sea. The young man was carrying a large fish speared through the back by a sort of trident. The excitement of this led the four of them to share a square yard of sand for a few minutes, making cautious overtures.

The next day, Tommy Rogers insisted that his wife should don mask and flippers and try the new sport. She was taken out into the bay, like a ship under escort, by the two men and young Betty Clarke. Mary Rogers did not like the suffocating feeling of the mask pressing against her nose. The speed the frog-feet lent her made her nervous, for she was not a strong swimmer. But she was not going to appear a coward with that young girl sporting along so easily just in front.

Out in the bay a small island, a mere cluster of warm red-brown rock, rose from a surf of frisking white. Around the island, a couple of feet below the surface, submerged rocks lay, and all over them floated the new race of frog-people, face down, tridents poised, observing the fish that darted there. As Mary looked back through her goggles to the shore, it seemed very far, and rather commonplace, with the striped umbrellas, the lolling browned bodies, the paddling children. That was the other sea. This was something different indeed. Here were the adventurers and explorers of the sea, who disdained the safe beaches.

Mary lay loose on the surface of the water and looked down. Enormous, this under-sea world, with great valleys and boulders, all waving green in the sun-dappled water. On a dazzling patch of white sand – twenty feet down, it seemed – sprouted green grass as fresh and bright as if it grew on the shore in sunlight. By reaching down her hand she could almost touch it. Further away, long fronds of weed rocked and swayed, a forest of them. Mary floated over them, feeling with repugnance how they reached up to touch her knees and shoulders with their soft dragging touch. Underneath her, now, a floor of rock, covered with thick growth. Pale grey-green shapes, swelling like balloons, or waving like streamers; delicate whitey-brown flowers and stars, bubbled silver with air; soft swelling udders or bladders of fine white film, all rocking and drifting in the slow under-sea movement. Mary was fascinated – a new world, this was. But also repelled. In her ears there was nothing but a splash and crash of surf, and, through it, voices that sounded a long way off. The rocks were now very close below. Suddenly, immediately below her, a thin brown arm reached down, groped in a dark gulf of rock, and pulled out a writhing tangle of grey-dappled flesh. Mary floundered up, slipping painfully on the rocks. She had drifted unknowingly close to the islet, and on the rocks above her stood a group of half-naked bronzed boys, yelling and screaming with excitement as they killed the octopus they had caught, by smashing it repeatedly against a great boulder. They would eat it – so Mary heard, for supper. No, it was too much. She was in a panic. The loathsome thing must have been six inches below her – she might have touched it! She climbed on to a rock, and looked for Tommy, who was lying on a rock fifty feet off, pointing down at something under it, while Francis Clarke dived for it, and then again. She saw him emerge with a small striped fish, while Tommy and Betty Clarke yelled their excitement.

But she looked at the octopus, which was now lying draped over a rock like a limp fringed grey rag; and called her husband, handed over the goggles, the flippers and the tube, and swam slowly back to shore.

There she stayed. Nothing would tempt her out again.

That day Tommy bought an under-water fish gun. Mary found herself thinking, first, that it was all very well to spend over five pounds on this bizarre equipment; and then, that they weren't going to have much fun at Christmas if they went on like this.

A couple of days passed. Mary was alone all day. Betty Clarke, apparently, was only a beach-widow when it suited her, for she much preferred the red-rock island to staying with Mary. Nevertheless, she did sometimes spend half an hour making conversation, and then, with a flurry of apology, darted off through the blue waves to rejoin the men.

Quite soon, Mary was able to say casually to Tommy: 'Only three days to go.'

'If only I'd tried this equipment earlier,' he said. 'Next year, I'll know better.'

But for some reason, the thought of next year did not enchant Mary. 'I don't think we ought to come here again,' she said. 'It's quite spoiled now it's so fashionable.'

'Oh well – anywhere, provided there's rocks and fish.'

On that next day, the two men and Betty Clarke were on the rock island from seven in the morning until lunchtime, to which meal they grudgingly allowed ten minutes, because it was dangerous to swim on a full stomach. Then they departed again until the darkness fell across the sea. All this time Mary Rogers lay on her towel on the beach, turning over and over in the sun. She was now a warm red gold all over. She imagined how Mrs Baxter would say: 'You've got yourself a fine tan!' And then, inevitably, 'You won't keep it long here, will you?' Mary found herself unaccountably close to tears. What did Tommy see in these people?

she asked herself. As for that young man Francis, she had never heard him make any remark that was not connected with the weights, the varieties or vagaries of fish!

That night, Tommy said he had asked the young couple to dinner at the Plaza.

'A bit rash, aren't you?'

'Oh well, let's have a proper meal, for once. Only another two days.'

Mary let that 'proper meal' pass. But she said: 'I shouldn't have thought they were the sort of people to make friends of.'

A cloud of irritation dulled his face. 'What's the matter with them?'

'In England, I don't think . . .'

'Oh come off it, Mary!'

In the big garden of the Plaza, where four years ago they had eaten three meals a day by right, they found themselves around a small table just over the sea. There was an orchestra and more waiters than guests, or so it seemed. Betty Clarke, seen for the first time out of a bathing costume, was revealed to be a remarkably pretty girl. Her thin brown shoulders emerged from a full white frock which Mary Rogers conceded to be not bad at all, and her wide blue eyes were bright in her brown face. Again Mary thought: If I were twenty – well, twenty-five years, younger, they'd take us for sisters.

As for Tommy, he looked as young as the young couple – it simply wasn't fair, thought Mary. She sat and listened while they talked of judging distances under water, and the advantages of various types of equipment.

They tried to draw her in; but there she sat, silent

and dignified. Francis Clarke, she had decided, looked stiff and commonplace in his suit, not at all the handsome young sea-god of the beaches. As for the girl, her giggle was irritating her.

They began to feel uncomfortable. Betty mentioned London, and the three conscientiously talked about London, while Mary said yes and no.

The young couple lived at Clapham, apparently; and they went into town for a show once a month.

'There's ever such a nice show running now,' said Betty. 'The one at the Princes.'

'We never get to a show these days,' said Tommy. 'It's five hours by train. Anyway, it's not in my line.'

'Speak for yourself,' said Mary.

'Oh I know you work in a matinée when you can.'

At the irritation in the look she gave him, the Clarkes involuntarily exchanged a glance; and Betty said tactfully, 'I like going to the theatre, it gives you something to talk about.'

Mary remained silent.

'My wife,' said Tommy, 'knows a lot about the theatre. She used to be in a theatre set – all that sort of thing.'

'Oh, how interesting!' said Betty eagerly.

Mary struggled with temptation, then fell. 'The man who did the décor for the show at the Princes used to have a villa here. We visited him quite a bit.'

Tommy gave his wife an alarmed and warning look, and said: 'I wish to God they wouldn't use so much garlic.'

'It's not much use coming to France,' said Mary, 'if you're going to be insular about food.'

'You never cook French at home,' said Tommy suddenly. 'Why not, if you like it so much?'

'How can I? If I do, you say you don't like your food messed up.'

'I can't stick garlic either,' said Betty, with an air of one confessing a crime. 'I must say I'm pleased to be back home where you can get a bit of good plain food.'

Tommy now looked in anxious appeal at his wife, but she enquired: 'Why don't you go to Brighton or somewhere like that?'

'Give me Brighton anytime,' said Francis Clarke. 'Or Cornwall. You can get damned good fishing off Cornwall. But Betty drags me here. France is over-rated, that's what I say.'

'It would really seem to be better if you stayed at home.'

But he was not going to be snubbed by Mary Rogers. 'As for the French,' he said aggressively, 'they think of nothing but their stomachs. If they're not eating, they're talking about it. If they spent half the time they spend on eating on something worth while, they could make something of themselves, that's what I say.'

'Such as – catching fish?'

'Well, what's wrong with that? Or . . . for instance . . .' Here he gave the matter his earnest consideration. 'Well. There's that Government of theirs for instance. They could do something about that.'

Betty, who was now flushed under her tan, rolled her blue eyes, and let out a high confused laugh. 'Oh, well you've got to consider what people say. France is so much the rage.'

A silence. It was to be hoped the awkward moment was over. But no; for Francis Clarke seemed to think matters needed clarifying. He said, with a sort of rallying gallantry towards his wife: 'She's got a bee in her bonnet about getting on.'

'Well,' cried Betty, 'it makes a good impression, you must admit that. And when Mr Beaker – Mr Beaker is his boss,' she explained to Mary, 'when you said to Mr Beaker at the whist drive you were going to the South of France, he was impressed, you can say what you like.'

Tommy offered his wife an entirely disloyal, sarcastic grin.

'A woman should think of her husband's career,' said Betty. 'It's true, isn't it? And I know I've helped Francis a lot. I'm sure he wouldn't have got that rise if it wasn't for making a good impression. Besides you meet such nice people. Last year, we made friends – well, acquaintance, if you like – with some people who live at Ealing. We wouldn't have, otherwise. He's in the films.'

'He's a cameraman,' said Francis, being accurate.

'Well, that's films, isn't it? And they asked us to a party. And who do you think was there?'

'Mr Beaker?' enquired Mary finely.

'How did you guess? Well, they could see, couldn't they? And I wouldn't be surprised if Francis couldn't be buyer, now they know he's used to foreigners. He should learn French, I tell him.'

'Can't speak a word,' said Francis. 'Can't stand it anyway, gabble, gabble, gabble.'

'Oh, but Mrs Rogers speaks it so beautifully,' cried Betty.

'She's cracked,' said Francis, goodhumouredly, nodding to indicate his wife. 'She spends half the year making clothes for three weeks' holiday at the sea. Then the other half making Christmas presents out of bits and pieces. That's all she ever does.'

'Oh, but it's so nice to give people presents with that individual touch,' said Betty.

'If you want to waste your time I'm not stopping you,' said Francis. 'I'm not stopping you. It's your funeral.'

'They're not grateful for what we do for them,' said Betty, wrestling with tears, trying to claim the older woman as an ally. 'If I didn't work hard, we couldn't afford the friends we've got . . .'

But Mary Rogers had risen from her place. 'I think I'm ready for bed,' she said. 'Goodnight, Mrs Clarke. Goodnight, Mr Clarke.' Without looking at her husband, she walked away.

Tommy Rogers hastily got up, paid the bill, bade the young couple an embarrassed good night, and hurried after his wife. He caught her up at the turning of the steep road up to the villa. The stars were brilliant overhead, the palms waved seductively in the soft breeze. 'I say,' he said angrily, 'that wasn't very nice of you.'

'I haven't any patience with that sort of thing,' said Mary. Her voice was high and full of tears. He looked at her in astonishment and held his peace.

But next day he went off to the fishing. For Mary, the holiday was over. She was packing and did not go to the beach.

That evening he said: 'They've asked us back to dinner.'

'You go. I'm tired.'

'I shall go,' he said defiantly, and went. He did not return until very late.

They had to catch the train early next morning. At the little station, they stood with their suitcases in a crowd of people who regretted the holiday was over. But Mary was regretting nothing. As soon as the train came in, she got in, and left Tommy shaking hands with crowds of English people whom apparently he had met the night before. At the last minute, the young Clarkes came running up in bathing costumes to say goodbye. She nodded stiffly out of the train window and went on arranging the baggage. Then the train started and her husband came in.

The compartment was full and there was an excuse not to talk. The silence persisted, however. Soon Tommy was watching her anxiously, and making remarks about the weather, which worsened steadily as they went north.

In Paris there were five hours to fill in.

They were walking beside the river, by the open-air market, when she stopped before a stall selling earthenware.

'That big bowl,' she exclaimed, her voice newly alive, 'that big red one, there – it would be just right for the Christmas tree.'

'So it would, go ahead and buy it, old girl,' he agreed at once, with infinite relief.

FLIGHT

Above the old man's head was the dovecote, a tall wire-netted shelf on stilts, full of strutting, preening birds. The sunlight broke on their grey breasts into small rainbows. His ears were lulled by their crooning, his hands stretched up towards his favourite, a homing pigeon, a young plumpbodied bird which stood still when it saw him and cocked a shrewd bright eye.

'Pretty, pretty, pretty,' he said, as he grasped the bird and drew it down, feeling the cold coral claws tighten around his finger. Content, he rested the bird lightly on his chest, and leaned against a tree, gazing out beyond the dovecote into the landscape of a late afternoon. In folds and hollows of sunlight and shade, the dark red soil, which was broken into great clods, stretched wide to a tall horizon. Trees marked the course of the valley; a stream of rich green grass the road.

His eyes travelled homewards along this road until he saw his granddaughter swinging on the gate underneath a frangipani tree. Her hair fell down her back in a wave of sunlight, and her long bare legs repeated the angles of the frangipani stems, bare, shining-brown stems among patterns of pale blossoms.

She was gazing past the pink flowers, past the railway

cottage where they lived, along the road to the village.

His mood shifted. He deliberately held out his wrist for the bird to take flight, and caught it again at the moment it spread its wings. He felt the plump shape strive and strain under his fingers; and, in a sudden access of troubled spite, shut the bird into a small box and fastened the bolt. 'Now you stay there,' he muttered; and turned his back on the shelf of birds. He moved warily along the hedge, stalking his granddaughter, who was now looped over the gate, her head loose on her arms, singing. The light happy sound mingled with the crooning of the birds, and his anger mounted.

'Hey!' he shouted; saw her jump, look back, and abandon the gate. Her eyes veiled themselves, and she said in a pert neutral voice: 'Hullo, Grandad.' Politely she moved towards him, after a lingering backward glance at the road.

'Waiting for Steven, hey?' he said, his fingers curling like claws into his palm.

'Any objection?' she asked lightly, refusing to look at him.

He confronted her, his eyes narrowed, shoulders hunched, tight in a hard knot of pain which included the preening birds, the sunlight, the flowers, herself. He said: 'Think you're old enough to go courting, hey?'

The girl tossed her head at the old-fashioned phrase and sulked, 'Oh, Grandad!'

'Think you want to leave home, hey? Think you can go running around the fields at night?'

Her smile made him see her, as he had every evening of this warm end-of-summer month, swinging hand in hand along the road to the village with that red-handed,

34

red-throated, violent-bodied youth, the son of the post-master. Misery went to his head and he shouted angrily: 'I'll tell your mother!'

'Tell away!' she said, laughing, and went back to the gate.

He heard her singing, for him to hear:

'I've got you under my skin,
I've got you deep in the heart of . . .'

'Rubbish,' he shouted. 'Rubbish. Impudent little bit of rubbish!'

Growling under his breath he turned towards the dovecote, which was his refuge from the house he shared with his daughter and her husband and their children. But now the house would be empty. Gone all the young girls with their laughter and their squabbling and their teasing. He would be left, uncherished and alone, with that square-fronted, calm-eyed woman, his daughter.

He stooped, muttering, before the dovecote, resenting the absorbed cooing birds.

From the gate the girl shouted: 'Go and tell! Go on, what are you waiting for?'

Obstinately he made his way to the house, with quick, pathetic persistent glances of appeal back at her. But she never looked around. Her defiant but anxious young body stung him into love and repentance. He stopped. 'But I never meant . . .' he muttered, waiting for her to turn and run to him. 'I didn't mean . . .'

She did not turn. She had forgotten him. Along the road came the young man Steven, with something in his hand. A present for her? The old man stiffened as he watched the gate swing back, and the couple embrace. In the brittle shadows of the frangipani tree his granddaughter, his darling, lay in the arms of the postmaster's son, and her hair flowered back over his shoulder.

'I see you!' shouted the old man spitefully. They did not move. He stumped into the little whitewashed house, hearing the wooden veranda creak angrily under his feet. His daughter was sewing in the front room, threading a needle held to the light.

He stopped again, looking back into the garden. The couple were now sauntering among the bushes, laughing. As he watched he saw the girl escape from the youth with a sudden mischievous movement, and run off through the flowers with him in pursuit. He heard shouts, laughter, a scream, silence.

'But it's not like that at all,' he muttered miserably. 'It's not like that. Why can't you see? Running and giggling, and kissing and kissing. You'll come to something quite different.'

He looked at his daughter with sardonic hatred, hating himself. They were caught and finished, both of them, but the girl was still running free.

'Can't you *see*?' he demanded of his invisible granddaughter, who was at that moment lying in the thick green grass with the postmaster's son.

His daughter looked at him and her eyebrows went up in tired forbearance.

'Put your birds to bed?' she asked, humouring him.

'Lucy,' he said urgently. 'Lucy . . .'

'Well, what is it now?'

'She's in the garden with Steven.'

'Now you just sit down and have your tea.'

He stumped his feet alternately, thump, thump, on the hollow wooden floor and shouted: 'She'll marry him. I'm telling you, she'll be marrying him next!'

His daughter rose swiftly, brought him a cup, set him a plate.

'I don't want any tea. I don't want it, I tell you.'

'Now, now,' she crooned. 'What's wrong with it? Why not?'

'She's eighteen. Eighteen!'

'I was married at seventeen and I never regretted it.'

'Liar,' he said. 'Liar. Then you should regret it. Why do you make your girls marry? It's you who do it. What do you do it for? Why?'

'The other three have done fine. They've three fine husbands. Why not Alice?'

'She's the last,' he mourned. 'Can't we keep her a bit longer?'

'Come, now, dad. She'll be down the road, that's all. She'll be here every day to see you.'

'But it's not the same.' He thought of the other three girls, transformed inside a few months from charming petulant spoiled children into serious young matrons.

'You never did like it when we married?' she said. 'Why not? Every time, it's the same. When I got married you made me feel like it was something wrong. And my girls the same. You get them all crying and miserable the way you go on. Leave Alice alone. She's happy.' She sighed, letting her eyes linger on the sun-lit garden. 'She'll marry next month. There's no reason to wait.'

'You've said they can marry?' he said incredulously.

'Yes, dad, why not?' she said coldly, and took up her sewing.

His eyes stung, and he went out on to the veranda. Wet spread down over his chin and he took out a handkerchief and mopped his whole face. The garden was empty.

From around a corner came the young couple; but their faces were no longer set against him. On the wrist of the postmaster's son balanced a young pigeon, the light gleaming on its breast.

'For me?' said the old man, letting the drops shake off his chin. 'For me?'

'Do you like it?' The girl grabbed his hand and swung on it. 'It's for you, Grandad. Steven brought it for you.' They hung about him, affectionate, concerned, trying to charm away his wet eyes and his misery. They took his arms and directed him to the shelf of birds, one on each side, enclosing him, petting him, saying wordlessly that nothing would be changed, nothing could change, and that they would be with him always. The bird was proof of it, they said, from their lying happy eyes, as they thrust it on him. 'There, Grandad, it's yours. It's for you.'

They watched him as he held it on his wrist, stroking its soft, sun-warmed back, watching the wings lift and balance.

'You must shut it up for a bit,' said the girl intimately. 'Until it knows this is its home.'

'Teach your grandmother to suck eggs,' growled the old man.

Released by his half-deliberate anger, they fell back, laughing at him. 'We're glad you like it.' They moved off, now serious and full of purpose, to the gate, where they hung, backs to him, talking quietly. More than anything could their grown-up seriousness shut him out, making him alone; also, it quietened him, took the sting out of their tumbling like puppies on the grass. They had forgotten him again. Well, so they should, the old man reassured himself, feeling his throat clotted with tears, his lips trembling. He held the new bird to his face, for the caress of its silken feathers. Then he shut it in a box and took out his favourite.

'*Now* you can go,' he said aloud. He held it poised, ready for flight, while he looked down the garden towards the boy and the girl. Then, clenched in the pain of loss, he lifted the bird on his wrist and watched it soar. A whirr and a spatter of wings, and a cloud of birds rose into the evening from the dovecote.

At the gate Alice and Steven forgot their talk and watched the birds.

On the veranda, that woman, his daughter, stood gazing, her eyes shaded with a hand that still held her sewing.

It seemed to the old man that the whole afternoon had stilled to watch his gesture of self-command, that even the leaves of the trees had stopped shaking.

Dry-eyed and calm, he let his hands fall to his side and stood erect, staring up into the sky.

The cloud of shining silver birds flew up and up, with a shrill cleaving of wings, over the dark ploughed land and the darker belts of trees and the bright folds of grass, until they floated high in the sunlight, like a cloud of motes of dust.

They wheeled in a wide circle, tilting their wings so there was flash after flash of light, and one after another they dropped from the sunshine of the upper sky to shadow, one after another, returned to the shadowed earth over trees and grass and field, returning to the valley and the shelter of night.

The garden was all a fluster and a flurry of returning birds. Then silence, and the sky was empty.

The old man turned, slowly, taking his time; he lifted

his eyes to smile proudly down the garden at his grand-daughter. She was staring at him. She did not smile. She was wide-eyed, and pale in the cold shadow, and he saw the tears run shivering off her face.

HOW I FINALLY LOST
MY HEART

It would be easy to say that I picked up a knife, slit open my side, took my heart out, and threw it away; but unfortunately it wasn't as easy as that. Not that I, like everyone else, had not often wanted to do it. No, it happened differently, and not as I expected.

It was just after I had had a lunch and a tea with two different men. My lunch partner I had lived with for (more or less) four and seven-twelfths years. When he left me for new pastures, I spent two years, or was it three? half-dead, and my heart was a stone, impossible to carry about, considering all the other things weighing on one. Then I slowly, and with difficulty, got free, because my heart cherished a thousand adhesions to my first love – though from another point of view he could be legitimately described as either my second *real* love (my father being the first), or my third (my brother intervening).

As the folk-song has it:

I have loved but three men in my life,
My father, my brother, and the man that
took my life.

But if one were going to look at the thing from outside, without insight, he could be seen as (perhaps, I forget) the thirteenth, but to do that means disregarding the inner emotional truth. For we all know that these affairs or entanglements one has between *serious* loves, though they may number dozens and stretch over years, *don't really count.*

This way of looking at things creates a number of unhappy people, for it is well known that what doesn't really count for me, might very well count for you. But there is no way of getting over this difficulty, for a *serious* love is the most important business in life, or nearly so. At any rate, most of us are engaged in looking for it. Even when we are, in fact, being very serious indeed with one person we still have an eighth of an eye cocked in case some stranger unexpectedly encountered might turn out to be even more serious. We are all entirely in agreement that we are in the right to taste, test, sip and sample a thousand people on our way to the *real* one. It is not too much to say that in our circles tasting and sampling is probably the second most important activity, the first being earning money. Or to put it another way, 'If you are serious about this thing, you go on laying everybody that offers until something clicks and you're all set to go.'

I have digressed from an earlier point: that I regarded this man I had lunch with (we will call him A) as my first love; and still do, despite the Freudians, who insist on seeing my father as A and possibly my brother as B, making my (real) first love C. And despite, also, those who might ask: What about your two husbands and all those affairs?

What about them? I did not *really* love them, the way I loved A.

I had lunch with him. Then, quite by chance, I had tea with B. When I say B, here, I mean my *second* serious love, not my brother, or the little boys I was in love with between the ages of five and fifteen, if we are going to take fifteen (arbitrarily) as the point of no return . . . which last phrase is in itself a pretty brave defiance of the secular arbiters.

In between A and B (my count) there were a good many affairs, or samples, but they didn't count. B and I *clicked*, we went off like a bomb, though not quite as simply as A and I had clicked, because my heart was bruised, sullen, and suspicious because of A's throwing me over. Also there were all those ligaments and adhesions binding me to A still to be loosened, one by one. However, for a time B and I got on like a house on fire, and then we came to grief. My heart was again a ton-weight in my side.

If this were a stone in my side, a stone,
I could pluck it out and be free . . .

Having lunch with A, then tea with B, two men who between them had consumed a decade of my precious years (I am not counting the test or trial affairs in between) and, it is fair to say, had balanced all the delight (plenty and intense) with misery (oh Lord, Lord) – moving from one to the other, in the course of an afternoon, conversing amiably about this and that, with meanwhile my heart giving no more than slight reminiscent tugs, the fish of memory at the end of a long slack line . . .

To sum up, it was salutary.

Particularly as that evening I was expecting to meet C, or someone who might very well turn out to be C –

though I don't want to give too much emphasis to C, the truth is I can hardly remember what he looked like, but one can't be expected to remember the unimportant ones one has sipped or tasted in between. But after all, he might have turned out to be C, we might have *clicked*, and I was in that state of mind (in which we all so often are) of thinking: He might turn out to be the one. (I use a woman's magazine phrase deliberately here, instead of saying, as I might: *Perhaps it will be serious*.)

So there I was (I want to get the details and atmosphere right) standing at a window looking into a street (Great Portland Street, as a matter of fact) and thinking that while I would not dream of regretting my affairs, or experiences, with A and B (it is better to have loved and lost than never to have loved at all) my anticipation of the heart because of spending an evening with a possible C had a certain unreality, because there was no doubt that both A and B had caused me unbelievable pain. Why, therefore, was I looking forward to C? I should rather be running away as fast as I could.

It suddenly occurred to me that I was looking at the whole phenomenon quite inaccurately. My (or perhaps I am permitted to say our?) way of looking at it is that one must search for an A, or a B, or a C or a D with a certain combination of desirable or sympathetic qualities so that one may click, or spontaneously combust: or to put it differently, one needs a person who, like a saucer of water, allows one to float off on him/her like a transfer. But this isn't so at all. Actually one carries with one a sort of burning spear stuck in one's side, that one waits for someone else to pull out; it is something painful, like a sore or a wound, that one cannot wait to share with someone else.

I saw myself quite plainly in a moment of truth: I was standing at a window (on the third floor) with A and B (to mention only the mountain peaks of my emotional experience) behind me, a rather attractive woman, if I may say so, with a mellowness that I would be the first to admit is the sad harbinger of age, but is attractive by definition, because it is a testament to the amount of sampling and sipping (I nearly wrote simpling and sapping) I have done in my time . . . there I stood, brushed, dressed, red-lipped, kohl-eyed, all waiting for an evening with a possible C. And at another window overlooking (I think I am right in saying) Margaret Street, stood C, brushed, washed, shaved, smiling: an attractive man (I think), and *he* was thinking: Perhaps she will turn out to be D (or A or 3 or ? or %, or whatever symbol he used). We stood, separated by space, but in identical conditions of pleasant uncertainty and anticipation, and we both held our hearts in our hands, all pink and palpitating and ready for pleasure and pain, and we were about to throw these hearts in each other's faces like snowballs, or cricketballs (How's that?) or, more accurately, like great bleeding wounds: 'Take my wound.' Because the last thing one ever thinks at such moments is that he (or she) will say: Take *my* wound, please remove the spear from *my* side, no, not at all, one simply expects to get rid of one's own.

I decided I must go to the telephone and say, C – you know that joke about the joke-makers who don't trouble to tell each other jokes, but simply say Joke 1, or Joke 2, and everyone roars with laughter, or snickers, or giggles appropriately . . . actually one could reverse the game by guessing whether it was joke C(b) or Joke A(d) according to what sort of laughter a

45

person made to match the silent thought . . . well, C (I imagined myself saying), the analogy is for our instruction: Let's take the whole thing as read or said. Let's not lick each other's sores; let's keep our hearts to ourselves. Because just consider it, C, how utterly absurd – here we stand at our respective windows with our palpitating hearts in our hands . . .

At this moment, dear reader, I was forced simply to put down the telephone with an apology. For I felt the fingers of my left hand push outwards around something rather large, light, and slippery – hard to describe this sensation, really. My hand is not large, and my heart was in a state of inflation after having had lunch with A, tea with B, and then looking forward to C . . . anyway, my fingers were stretching out rather desperately to encompass an unknown, largish, lightish object, and I said Excuse me a minute, to C, looked down, and there was my heart, in my hand.

I had to end the conversation there.

For one thing, to find that one has achieved something so often longed for, so easily, is upsetting. It's not as if I had been trying. To get something one wants simply by accident – no, there's no pleasure in it, no feeling of achievement. So to find myself heart-whole, or, more accurately, heart-less, or at any rate, rid of the damned thing, and at such an awkward moment, in the middle of an imaginary telephone call with a man who might possibly turn out to be C, well it was irritating rather than not.

For another thing, a heart, raw and bleeding and fresh from one's side is not the prettiest sight. I'm not going into that at all. I was appalled, and indeed embarrassed that *that* was what had been loving and beating

46

away all those years, because if I'd had any idea at all
– well, enough of that.

My problem was, how to get rid of it.

Simple, you'll say, drop it into the waste-bucket.

Well, let me tell you, that's what I tried to do, I took
a good look at this object, nearly died with embarrassment, and walked over to the rubbish can, where I tried
to let it roll off my fingers. It wouldn't. It was stuck.
There was my heart, a large red pulsing bleeding repulsive object, stuck to my fingers. What was I going to
do? I sat down, lit a cigarette (with one hand, holding
the matchbox between my knees), held my hand with
the heart stuck on it over the side of the chair so that
it could drip into a bucket, and considered.

If this were a stone in my hand, a stone,
I could throw it over a tree . . .

When I had finished the cigarette, I carefully
unwrapped some tinfoil, of the kind used to wrap food
in when cooking, and I fitted a sort of cover around
my heart. This was absolutely and urgently necessary.
First, it was smarting badly. After all, it had spent some
forty years protected by flesh and ribs and the air was
too much for it. Secondly, I couldn't have any Tom,
Dick and Harry walking in and looking at it. Thirdly,
I could not look at it for too long myself, it filled me
with shame. The tinfoil was effective, and indeed rather
striking. It is quite pliable and now it seemed as if there
were a stylized heart balanced on my palm, like a globe,
in glittering, silvery substance. I almost felt I needed a
sceptre in the other hand to balance it . . . But the
thing was, there is no other word for it, in bad taste. I
then wrapped a scarf around hand and tinfoiled heart,

47

and felt safer. Now it was a question of pretending to have hurt my hand until I could think of a way of getting rid of my heart altogether, short of amputating my hand.

Meanwhile I telephoned (really, not in imagination) C, who now would never be C. I could feel my heart, which was stuck so close to my fingers that I could feel every beat or tremor, give a gulp of resigned grief at the idea of this beautiful experience now never to be. I told him some idiotic lie about having 'flu. Well, he was all stiff and indignant, but concealing it urbanely, as I would have done, making a joke but allowing a tiny barb of sarcasm to rankle in the last well-chosen phrase. Then I sat down again to think out my whole situation.

There I sat.

What was I going to do?

There I sat.

I am going to have to skip about four days here, viral enough in all conscience, because I simply cannot go heart-beat by heart-beat through my memories. A pity, since I suppose this is what this story is about; but in brief: I drew the curtains, I took the telephone off the hook, I turned on the lights, I took the scarf off the glittering shape, then the tinfoil, then I examined the heart. There were two-fifths of a century's experiences to work through, and before I had even got through the first night, I was in a state hard to describe . . .

Or if I could pull the nerves from my skin
A quick red net to drag through a sea for fish . . .

By the end of the fourth day I was worn out. By no act of will, or intention, or desire could I move that heart by a fraction – on the contrary, it was not only stuck to my fingers, like a sucked boiled sweet, but was actually growing to the flesh of my fingers and my palm.

I wrapped it up again in tinfoil and scarf, and turned out the lights and pulled up the blinds and opened the curtains. It was about ten in the morning, an ordinary London day, neither hot nor cold nor clear nor clouded nor wet nor fine. And while the street is interesting, it is not exactly beautiful, so I wasn't looking at it so much as waiting for something to catch my attention while thinking of something else.

Suddenly I heard a tap-tap tapping that got louder, sharp and clear, and I knew before I saw her that this was the sound of high heels on a pavement though it might just as well have been a hammer against stone. She walked fast opposite my window and her heels hit the pavement so hard that all the noises of the street seemed absorbed into that single tap-tap clang-clang. As she reached the corner at Great Portland Street two London pigeons swooped diagonally from the sky very fast, as if they were bullets aimed to kill her; and then as they saw her they swooped up and off at an angle. Meanwhile, she had turned the corner. All this has taken time to write down, but the thing happening took a couple of seconds: the woman's body hitting the pavement bang-bang through her heels then sharply turning the corner in a right-angle; and the pigeons making another acute angle across hers and intersecting it in a fast sweep of displaced air. Nothing to all that, of course, nothing – she had gone off down the street, her heels tip-tapping, and the pigeons landed on my window-sill and began cooing. All gone, all vanished, the marvellous exact co-ordination of sound and movement, but it had happened, it had made me happy and exhilarated, I had no problems in this world, and I realized that the heart stuck to my fingers was quite loose. I couldn't get it off altogether, though I was tugging at it under the scarf and the tinfoil, but almost.

I understood that sitting and analysing each movement or pulse or beat of my heart through forty years was a mistake. I was on the wrong track altogether: this was the way to attach my red, bitter, delighted heart to my flesh for ever and ever . . .

Ha! So you think I'm done! You think . . .
Watch, I'll roll my heart in a mesh of rage
And bounce it like a handball off
Walls, faces, railings, umbrellas and pigeons'
backs –

No, all that was no good at all, it just made things worse. What I must do is to take myself by surprise, as it were, the way I was taken by surprise over the woman and the pigeons and the sharp sounds of heels and silk wings.

I put on my coat, held my lumpy scarfed arm across my chest, so that if anyone said: What have you done with your hand? I could say: I've banged my finger in the door. Then I walked down into the street.

It wasn't easy to go among so many people, when I was worried that they were thinking: What has that woman done to her hand; because that made it hard to forget myself. And all the time it tingled and throbbed against my fingers, reminding me.

Now I was out I didn't know what to do. Should I go and have lunch with someone? Or wander in the park? Or buy myself a dress? I decided to go to the Round Pond, and walk around it by myself. I was tired after four days and nights without sleep. I went down into the Underground at Oxford Circus. Midday. Crowds of people. I felt self-conscious, but of course need not have worried. I swear you could walk naked down the street in London and no one would even turn round.

So I went down the escalator and looked at the faces coming up past me on the other side, as I always do; and wondered, as I always do, how strange it is that those people and I should meet by chance in such a way, and how odd that we would never see each other again, or, if we did, we wouldn't know it. And I went on to the crowded platform and looked at the faces as I always do, and got into the train, which was very full, and found a seat. It wasn't as bad as at rush-hour, but all the seats were filled. I leaned back and closed my eyes, deciding to sleep a little, being so tired. I was just beginning to doze off, when I heard a woman's voice muttering, or rather, declaiming:

'A gold cigarette case, well, that's a nice thing, isn't it, I must say a gold case, yes . . .'

There was something about this voice which made me open my eyes: on the other side of the compartment, about eight persons away, sat a youngish woman, wearing a cheap green cloth coat, gloveless hands, flat brown shoes, and lisle stockings. She must be rather poor – a woman dressed like this is a rare sight, these days. But it was her posture that struck me. She was sitting half-twisted in her seat, so that her head was turned over her left shoulder, and she was looking straight at the stomach of an elderly man next to her. But it was clear

51

she was not seeing it: her young staring eyes were sightless, she was looking inwards.

She was so clearly alone, in the crowded compartment, that it was not as embarrassing as it might have been. I looked around, and people were smiling, or exchanging glances, or winking, or ignoring her, according to their natures, but she was oblivious of us all.

She suddenly aroused herself, turned so that she sat straight in her seat, and directed her voice and her gaze to the opposite seat:

'Well, so that's what you think, you think that, you think that do you, well, you think I'm just going to wait at home for you, but you gave her a gold case and . . .'

And with a clockwork movement of her whole thin person, she turned her narrow pale-haired head sideways over her left shoulder, and resumed her stiff empty stare at the man's stomach. He was grinning uncomfortably. I leaned forward to look along the line of people in the row of seats I sat in, and the man opposite her, a young man, had exactly the same look of discomfort which he was determined to keep amused. So we all looked at her, the young, thin, pale woman in her private drama of misery, who was so completely unconscious of us that she spoke and thought out loud. And, again, without particular warning or reason, in between stops, so it wasn't that she was disturbed from her dream by the train stopping at Bond Street, and then jumping forward again, she twisted her body frontways, and addressed the seat opposite her (the young man had got off, and a smart grey-curled matron had got in) –

'Well I know about it now, don't I, and if you come in all smiling and pleased, well then I know, don't I. You don't have to tell me, I know, and I've said to her, I've said, I know he gave you a gold cigarette case . . .'

At which point, with the same clockwork impulse, she stopped, or was checked, or simply ran out, and turned herself half around to stare at the stomach – the same stomach, for the middle-aged man was still there. But we stopped at Marble Arch and he got out, giving the compartment, rather than the people in it, a tolerant half-smile which said: I am sure I can trust you to realize that this unfortunate woman is stark staring mad . . .

His seat remained empty. No people got in at Marble Arch, and the two people standing waiting for seats did not want to sit by her to receive her stare.

We all sat, looking gently in front of us, pretending to ourselves and to each other that we didn't know the poor woman was mad and that, in fact, we ought to be doing something about it. I even wondered what I should say: Madam, you're mad, shall I escort you to your home? Or: Poor thing, don't go on like that, it doesn't do any good, you know – just leave him, that'll bring him to his senses . . .

And, behold, after the interval that was regulated by her inner mechanism had elapsed, she turned back and said to the smart matron who received this statement of accusation with perfect self-command:

'Yes, I know! Oh, yes! And what about my shoes, what about them, a golden cigarette case is what she got, the filthy bitch, a golden case . . .'

Stop. Twist. Stare. At the empty seat by her.

Extraordinary. Because it was a frozen misery, how shall I put it? A passionless passion – we were seeing unhappiness embodied, we were looking at the essence of some private tragedy – rather, Tragedy. There was no emotion in it. She was like an actress doing Accusation, or Betrayed Love, or Infidelity, when she had only just learned her lines and is not bothering to do more than get them right.

And whether she sat in her half-twisted position, her unblinking eyes staring at the greenish, furry, ugly covering of the train-seat, or sat straight, directing her accusation to the smart woman opposite, there was a frightening immobility about her – yes, that was why she frightened us. For it was clear that she might very well (if the inner machine ran down) stay silent, for ever, in either twisted or straight position, or at any point between them – yes we could all imagine her, frozen perpetually in some arbitrary pose. It was as if we watched the shell of some woman going through certain predetermined motions.

For *she* was simply not there. *What* was there, who she was, it was impossible to tell, though it was easy to imagine her thin, gentle little face breaking into a smile in total forgetfulness of what she was enacting now. She did not know she was in a train between Marble Arch and Queensway, nor that she was publicly accusing her husband or lover, nor that we were looking at her.

And we, looking at her, felt an embarrassment and shame that was not on her account at all . . .

Suddenly I felt, under the scarf and the tinfoil, a lightening of my fingers, as my heart rolled loose.

I hastily took it off my palm, in case it decided to adhere there again, and I removed the scarf, leaving balanced on my knees a perfect stylized heart, like a silver heart on a Valentine card, though of course it was three-dimensional. This heart was not so much harmless, no that isn't the word, as artistic, but in very bad taste, as I said. I could see that the people in the train, now looking at me and the heart, and not at the poor mad woman, were pleased with it.

I got up, took the four or so paces to where she was, and laid the tinfoil heart down on the seat so that it received her stare.

For a moment she did not react, then with a groan or a mutter of relieved and entirely theatrical grief, she leaned forward, picked up the glittering heart, and clutched it in her arms, hugging it and rocking it back and forth, even laying her cheek against it, while staring over its top at her husband as if to say: Look what I've got, I don't care about you and your cigarette case, I've got a silver heart.

I got up, since we were at Notting Hill Gate, and, followed by the pleased congratulatory nods and smiles of the people left behind, I went out on to the platform, up the escalators, into the street, and along to the park.

No heart. No heart at all. What bliss. What freedom . . .

Hear that sound? That's laughter, yes.
That's me laughing, yes, that's me.

ENGLAND VERSUS ENGLAND

'I think I'll be off,' said Charlie. 'My things are packed.'
He had made sure of getting his holdall ready so that
his mother wouldn't. 'But it's early,' she protested. Yet
she was already knocking red hands together to rid
them of water while she turned to say good-bye: she
knew her son was leaving early to avoid the father. But
the back door now opened and Mr Thornton came in.
Charlie and his father were alike: tall, over-thin, big-
boned. The old miner stooped, his hair had gone into
grey wisps, and his hollow cheeks were coal-pitted. The
young man was still fresh, with jaunty fair hair and alert
eyes. But there were scoops of strain under his eyes.

'You're alone,' said Charlie involuntarily, pleased,
ready to sit down again. The old man was not alone.
Three men came into view behind him in the light that
fell into the yard from the door, and Charlie said
quickly: 'I'm off, Dad, it's good-bye till Christmas.'
They all came crowding into the little kitchen, bringing
with them the spirit of facetiousness that seemed to
Charlie his personal spiteful enemy, like a poltergeist
standing in wait somewhere behind his right shoulder.
'So you're back to the dreaming spires,' said one man,
nodding good-bye. 'Off to t'palaces of learning,' said
another. Both were smiling. There was no hostility in

56

it, or even envy, but it shut Charlie out of his family away from his people. The third man, adding his tribute to this, the most brilliant son of the village, said: 'You'll be coming back to a right Christmas with us, then, or will you be frolicking with t'lords and t'earls you're the equal of now?'

'He'll be home for Christmas,' said the mother sharply. She turned her back on them, and dropped potatoes one by one from a paper bag into a bowl.

'For a day or so, any road,' said Charlie, in obedience to the prompting spirit. 'That's time enough to spend with t'hewers of wood and t'drawers of water.' The third man nodded, as if to say: That's right! and put back his head to let out a relieved bellow. The father and the other two men guffawed with him. Young Lennie pushed and shoved Charlie encouragingly and Charlie jostled back, while the mother nodded and smiled because of the saving horse-play. All the same, he had not been home for nearly a year, and when they stopped laughing and stood waiting for him to go, their grave eyes said they were remembering this fact.

'Sorry I've not had more time with you, son,' said Mr Thornton, 'but you know how 'tis.'

The old miner had been union secretary, was now chairman and had spent his working life as miners' representative in a dozen capacities. When he walked through the village, men at a back-door, or a woman in an apron, called: 'Just a minute, Bill,' and came after him. Every evening Mr Thornton sat in the kitchen, or in the parlour when the television was claimed by the children, giving advice about pensions, claims, work-rules, allowances; filling in forms; listening to tales of trouble. Ever since Charlie could remember, Mr Thornton had been less his father than the father of the village. Now the three miners went into the parlour, and Mr Thornton laid his hand on his son's shoulder, and said: 'It's been good seeing you,' nodded and followed them. As he shut the door he said to his wife: 'Make us a cup of tea, will you, lass?'

'There's time for a cup, Charlie,' said the mother, meaning there was no need for him to rush off now, when it was unlikely any more neighbours would come in. Charlie did not hear. He was watching her slosh dirty potatoes about under the running tap while with her free hand she reached for the kettle. He went to fetch his raincoat and his holdall listening to the nagging inner voice which he hated, but which he felt as his only protection against the spiteful enemy outside: 'I can't stand it when my father apologizes to me – he was apologizing to me for not seeing more of me. If he wasn't as he is, better than anyone else in the village, and our home the only house with real books in it, I wouldn't be at Oxford. I wouldn't have done well at school, so it cuts both ways.' The words, cuts both ways, echoed uncannily in his inner ear, and he felt queasy, as if the earth he stood on was shaking. His eyes cleared on the sight of his mother, standing in front of him, her shrewd, non-judging gaze on his face. 'Eh, lad,' she said. 'You don't look any too good to me.' 'I'm all right,' he said hastily, and kissed her, adding: 'Say my piece to the girls when they come in.' He went out, with Lennie behind him.

The two youths walked in silence past fifty crammed lively brightly-lit kitchens whose doors kept opening as the miners came in from the pit for their tea. They walked in silence along the fronts of fifty more houses. The fronts were all dark. The life of the village, even now, was in the kitchens where great fires roared all day on the cheap coal. The village had been built in the thirties by the company, now nationalized. There were two thousand houses, exactly alike, with identical patches of carefully tended front garden, and busy back-yards. Nearly every house had a television aerial. From every chimney poured black smoke.

At the bus stop Charlie turned to look back at the village, now a low hollow of black, streaked and splattered with sullen wet lights. He tried to isolate the gleam from his own home, while he thought how he loved his home and how he hated the village. Everything about it offended him, yet as soon as he stepped inside his kitchen he was received into warmth. That morning he had stood on the front step and looked out on lines of grey stucco houses on either side of grey tarmac; on grey ugly lamp-posts and greyish hedges, and beyond to the grey mine-tip and the neat black diagram of the mine-head.

He had looked, listening while the painful inner voice lectured: 'There's nothing in sight, not one object or building anywhere, that is beautiful. Everything is so ugly and mean and graceless that it should be bulldozed into the earth and out of the memory of man.' There was not even a cinema. There was a post office, and attached to it a library that had romances and war stories. There were two miners' clubs for drinking. And there was television. These were the amenities for two thousand families.

When Mr Thornton stood on his front step and looked forth he smiled with pride and called his children to say: 'You've never seen what a miners' town can be like. You couldn't even imagine the conditions. Slums, that's what they used to be. Well, we've put an end to all that . . . Yes, off you go to Doncaster, I suppose, dancing and the pictures – that's all you can think about. And you take it all for granted. Now, in our time . . .'

And so, when Charlie visited his home, he was careful that none of his bitter criticisms reached words for, above all, he could not bear to hurt his father.

A group of young miners came along for the bus. They wore smartly-shouldered suits, their caps set at angles, and scarves flung back over their shoulders. They greeted Lennie, looked to see who the stranger was, and when Lennie said: 'This is my brother,' they nodded and turned quickly to board the bus. They went upstairs, and Lennie and Charlie went to the front downstairs. Lennie looked like them, with a strong cloth cap and jaunty scarf. He was short, stocky, strong – 'built for t'pit,' Mr Thornton said. But Lennie was in a foundry in Doncaster. No pit for him, he said. He had heard his father coughing through all the nights of his childhood, and the pit wasn't for him. But he had never said this to his father.

Lennie was twenty. He earned seventeen pounds a week, and wanted to marry a girl he had been courting for three years now. But he could not marry until the big brother was through college. The father was still on the coal-face, when by rights of age he should have been on the surface, because he earned four pounds a week more on the face. The sister in the office had wanted to be a school-teacher, but at the moment of decision all the extra money of the family had been needed for Charlie. It cost them two hundred pounds a year for his extras at Oxford. The only members of the family not making sacrifices for Charlie were the schoolgirl and the mother.

It was half an hour on the bus, and Charlie's muscles

were set hard in readiness for what Lennie might say, which must be resisted. Yet he had come home thinking: Well, at least I can talk it out with Lennie, I can be honest with him.

Now Lennie said facetiously, but with an anxious loving inspection of his brother's face: 'And what for do we owe the pleasure of your company, Charlie boy? You could have knocked us all down with a feather when you said you were coming this week-end.'

Charlie said angrily: 'I got fed up with t'earls and t'dukes.'

'Eh,' said Lennie quickly, 'but you didn't need to mind *them*, they didn't mean to rile you.'

'I know they didn't.'

'Mum's right,' said Lennie, with another anxious, but carefully brief glance, 'you're not looking too good, what's up?'

'What if I don't pass t'examinations,' said Charlie in a rush.

'Eh, but what is this, then? You were always first in school. You were the best of everyone. Why shouldn't you pass, then?'

'Sometimes I think I won't,' said Charlie lamely, but glad he had let the moment pass.

Lennie examined him again, this time frankly, and gave a movement like a shrug. But it was a hunching of the shoulders against a possible defeat. He sat hunched, his big hands on his knees. On his face was a small critical grin. Not critical of Charlie, not at all, but of life.

His heart beating painfully with guilt Charlie said: 'It's not as bad as that, I'll pass.' The inner enemy remarked softly: 'I'll pass, then I'll get a nice pansy job in a publisher's office with the other wet-nosed little

boys, or I'll be a sort of clerk. Or I'll be a teacher –
I've no talent for teaching, but what's that matter? Or
I'll be on the management side of industry, pushing
people like Lennie around. And the joke is, Lennie's
earning more than I shall for years.' The enemy behind
his right shoulder began satirically tolling a bell and
intoned: 'Charlie Thornton, in his third year at Oxford,
was found dead in a gas-filled bed-sitting-room this
morning. He had been overworking. Death from natural causes.' The enemy added a loud rude raspberry
and fell silent. But he was waiting: Charlie could feel
him there waiting.

Lennie said: 'Seen a doctor, Charlie-boy?'

'Yes. He said I should take it easy a bit. That's why
I came home.'

'No point killing yourself working.'

'No, it's not serious, he just said I must take it easy.'

Lennie's face remained grave. Charlie knew that
when he got home he would say to the mother: 'I think
Charlie's got summat on his mind.' And his mother
would say (while she stood shaking chips of potato into
boiling fat): 'I expect sometimes he wonders, is the
grind worth it? And he sees you earning, when he isn't.'
She would say, after a silence during which they
exchanged careful looks: 'It must be hard for him,
coming here, everything different, then off he goes,
everything different again.'

'Shouldn't worry, mum.'

'I'm not worrying. Charlie's all right.'

The inner voice inquired anxiously: 'If she's on the
spot about the rest, I suppose she's right about the last
bit too, *I suppose I am all right*?'

But the enemy behind his right shoulder said: 'A

man's best friend is his mother, she never lets a thing pass.'

Last year he had brought Jenny down for a week-end, to satisfy the family's friendly curiosity about the posh people he knew these days. Jenny was a poor clergyman's daughter, bookish, a bit of a prig, but a nice girl. She had easily navigated the complicated currents of the week-end, while the family waited for her to put on 'side'. Afterwards Mrs Thornton had said, putting her finger on the sore spot: 'That's a right nice girl. She's a proper mother to you, and that's a fact.' The last was not a criticism of the girl, but of Charlie. Now Charlie looked with envy at Lennie's responsible profile and said to himself: Yes, he's a man. He has been for years, since he left school. Me, I'm a proper baby, and I've got two years over him.

For, above everything else, Charlie was made to feel, every time he came home, that these people, his people were serious; while he and the people with whom he would now spend his life (if he passed the examination) were not serious. He did not believe this. The inner didactic voice made short work of any such idea. The outer enemy could, and did, parody it in a hundred ways. His family did not believe it, they were proud of him. Yet Charlie felt it in everything they said and did. They protected him. They sheltered him. And, above all, they still paid for him. At his age, his father had been working in the pit for eight years.

Lennie would be married next year. He already talked of a family. He, Charlie (if he passed the examination), would be running around licking people's arses to get a job, Bachelor of Arts, Oxford, and a drug on the market.

They had reached Doncaster. It was raining. Soon

they would pass where Doreen, Lennie's girl, worked. 'You'd better get off here,' Charlie said. 'You'll have all that drag back through the wet.' 'No, s'all right, I'll come with you to the station.'

There were another five minutes to go. 'I don't think it's right, the way you get at mum,' Lennie said, at last coming to the point.

'But I haven't said a bloody word,' said Charlie, switching without having intended it into his other voice, the middle-class voice which he was careful never to use with his family except in joke. Lennie gave him a glance of surprise and reproach and said: 'All the same. She feels it.'

'But it's bloody ridiculous.' Charlie's voice was rising. 'She stands in that kitchen all day, pandering to our every whim, when she's not doing housework or making a hundred trips a day with that bloody coal . . .' In the Christmas holidays, when Charlie had visited home last, he had fixed up a bucket on the frame of an old pram to ease his mother's work. This morning he had seen the contrivance collapsed and full of rainwater in the back-yard. After breakfast Lennie and Charlie had sat at the table in their shirt-sleeves watching their mother. The door was open into the backyard. Mrs Thornton carried a shovel whose blade was nine inches by ten, and was walking back and forth from the coal-hole in the yard, through the kitchen, into the parlour. On each inward journey, a small clump of coal balanced on the shovel. Charlie counted that his mother walked from the coal-hole to the kitchen fire and the parlour fire thirty-six times. She walked steadily, the shovel in front, held like a spear in both hands, and her face frowned with purpose. Charlie had dropped his head on to his arms and laughed soundlessly until he felt Lennie's warning gaze and stopped the heave of his shoulders. After a moment he had sat up, straight-faced. Lennie said: 'Why do you get at mum, then?' Charlie said: 'But I haven't said owt.' 'No, but she's getting riled. You always show what you think, Charlie-boy.' As Charlie did not respond to this appeal – for far more than present charity, Lennie went on: 'You can't teach an old dog new tricks.' 'Old! She's not fifty!'

Now Charlie said, continuing the early conversation: 'She goes on as if she were an old woman. She wears herself out with nothing – she could get through all the work she has in a couple of hours if she organized herself. Or if just for once she told us where to get off.'

'What'd she do with herself, then?'

'Do? Well she could do something for herself. Read. Or see friends. Or something.'

'She feels it. Last time you went off she cried.'

'She *what*?' Charlie's guilt almost overpowered him, but the inner didactic voice switched on in time and he spoke through it. 'What right have we to treat her like a bloody servant? Betty likes her food this way and that way, and Dad won't eat this and that, and she stands there and humours the lot of us – like a servant.'

'And who was it last night said he wouldn't have fat on his meat and changed it for hers?' said Lennie smiling, but full of reproach.

'Oh, I'm just as bad as the rest of you,' said Charlie, sounding false. 'It makes me wild to see it,' he said, sounding sincere. Didactically he said: 'All the women in the village – they take it for granted. If someone organized them so that they had half a day to themselves sometimes, they'd think they were being insulted – they can't stop working. Just look at mum, then. She comes into Doncaster to wrap sweets two or three times a week – well, she actually loses money on it, by the time she's paid bus fares. I said to her, you're actually losing money on it, and she said: I like to get out and see a bit of life. A bit of life! Wrapping sweets in a bloody factory. Why can't she just come into town of an evening and have a bit of fun without feeling she has to pay for it by wrapping sweets, sweated bloody labour, and she actually loses on it. It doesn't make sense. They're human beings, aren't they, not just . . .'

'Not just what?' asked Lennie angrily. He had listened to Charlie's tirade, his mouth setting harder, his eyes narrowing. 'Here's the station,' he said in relief. They waited for the young miners to clatter down and off before going forward themselves. 'I'll come with you to your stop,' said Charlie; and they crossed the dark, shiny, grimy street to the opposite stop for the bus which would take Lennie back to Doreen.

'It's no good thinking we're going to change, Charlie-boy.'

'Who said change?' said Charlie excitedly; but the bus had come, and Lennie was already swinging on to the back. 'If you're in trouble just write and say,' said Lennie, and the bell pinged and his face vanished as the lit bus was absorbed by the light-streaked drizzling darkness.

There was half an hour before the London train. Charlie stood with the rain on his shoulders, his hands in his pockets, wondering whether to go after his brother and explain – what? He bolted across the street to the pub near the station. It was run by an Irishman who knew him and Lennie. The place was still empty, being just after opening time.

'It's you, then,' said Mike, drawing him a pint of

bitter without asking. 'Yes, it's me,' said Charlie, swinging himself up on to a stool.

'And what's in the great world of learning?'

'Oh Jesus, *no*!' said Charlie. The Irishman blinked, and Charlie said quickly: 'What have you gone and tarted this place up for?'

The pub had been panelled in dark wood. It was ugly and comforting. Now it had half a dozen bright wallpapers and areas of shining paint, and Charlie's stomach moved again, light filled his eyes, and he set his elbows hard down for support, and put his chin on his two fists.

'The youngsters like it,' said the Irishman. 'But we've left the bar next door as it was for the old ones.'

'You should have a sign up: Age This Way,' said Charlie. 'I'd have known where to go.' He carefully lifted his head off his fists, narrowing his eyes to exclude the battling colours of the wallpapers, the shine of the paint.

'You look bad,' said the Irishman. He was a small, round, alcoholically cheerful man who, like Charlie, had two voices. For the enemy – that is, all the English whom he did not regard as a friend, which meant people who were not regulars – he put on an exaggerated brogue which was bound, if he persisted, to lead to the political arguments he delighted in. For friends like Charlie he didn't trouble himself. He now said: 'All work and no play.'

'That's right,' said Charlie. 'I went to the doctor. He gave me a tonic and said I am fundamentally sound in wind and limb. "You are sound in wind and limb," he said,' said Charlie, parodying an upper-class English voice for the Irishman's pleasure.

Mike winked, acknowledging the jest, while his

professionally humorous face remained serious. 'You can't burn the candle at both ends,' he said in earnest warning.

Charlie laughed out. 'That's what the doctor said. "You can't burn the candle at both ends," he said.'

This time, when the stool he sat on, and the floor beneath the stool, moved away from him, and the glittering ceiling dipped and swung, his eyes went dark and stayed dark. He shut them and gripped the counter tight. With his eyes still shut he said facetiously: 'It's the clash of cultures, that's what it is. It makes me light-headed.' He opened his eyes and saw from the Irishman's face that he had not said these words aloud.

He said aloud: 'Actually the doctor was all right, he meant well. But, Mike, I'm not going to make it, I'm going to fail.'

'Well, it won't be the end of the world.'

'*Jesus*. That's what I like about you, Mike, you take a broad view of life.'

'I'll be back,' said Mike, going to serve a customer.

A week ago Charlie had gone to the doctor with a cyclostyled leaflet in his hand. It was called: A Report Into the Increased Incidence of Breakdown Among Undergraduates. He had underlined the words: 'Young men from working-class and lower middle-class families on scholarships are particularly vulnerable. For them, the gaining of a degree is obviously crucial. In addition they are under the continuous strain of adapting themselves to middle-class mores that are foreign to them. They are victims of a clash of standards, a clash of cultures, divided loyalties.'

The doctor, a young man of about thirty, provided by the college authorities as a sort of father-figure to advise on work problems, personal problems and (as the satirical *alter ego* took pleasure in pointing out) on clash-of-culture problems, glanced once at the pamphlet and handed it back. He had written it. As, of course, Charlie had known. 'When are your examinations?' he asked. *Getting to the root of the matter, just like mum*, remarked the malevolent voice from behind Charlie's shoulder.

'I've got five months, Doctor, and I can't work and I can't sleep.'

'For how long?'

'It's been coming on gradually.' *Ever since I was born*, said the enemy.

'I can give you sedatives and sleeping pills, of course, but that's not going to touch what's really wrong.'

Which is, all this unnatural mixing of the classes. Doesn't do, you know. People should know their place and stick to it. 'I'd like some sleep-pills, all the same.'

'Have you got a girl?'

'Two.'

The doctor paid out an allowance of man-of-the-world sympathy, then shut off his smile and said: 'Perhaps you'd be better with one?'

Which, my mum-figure, or my lovely bit of sex? – 'Perhaps I would, at that.'

'I could arrange for you to have some talks with a psychiatrist – well, not if you don't want,' he said hastily, for the *alter ego* had exploded through Charlie's lips in a horse-laugh and: 'What can the trick-cyclist tell me I don't know?' He roared with laughter, flinging his legs up; and an ashtray went circling around the room on its rim. Charlie laughed, watched the ashtray, and thought: There, I knew all the time it was a poltergeist sitting there behind my shoulder. I swear I never touched that damned ashtray.

The doctor waited until it circled near him, stopped it with his foot, picked it up, laid it back on the desk. 'It's no point your going to him if you feel like that.'

All avenues explored, all roads charted.

'Well now, let's see, have you been to see your family recently?'

'Last Christmas. No, Doctor, it's not because I don't want to, it's because I can't work there.' *You try working in an atmosphere of trade union meetings and telly and the pictures in Doncaster. You try it, Doc. And, besides, all my energies go into not upsetting them. Because I do upset them. My dear Doc, when we scholarship boys jump our class, it's not we who suffer, it's our families. We are an expense, Doc. And besides – write a thesis, I'd like to read it . . . call it: Long-term effects on working-class or lower middle-class family of a scholarship child whose existence is a perpetual reminder that they are nothing but ignorant non-cultured clods. How's that for a thesis, Doc? Why, I do believe I could write it myself.*

'If I were you, I'd go home for a few days. Don't try to work at all. Go to the pictures. Sleep and eat and let them fuss over you. Get this prescription made up and come and see me when you get back.'

'Thanks, Doc, I will.' *You mean well.*

The Irishman came back to find Charlie spinning a penny, so intent on this game that he did not see him. First he spun it with his right hand, anti-clockwise, then with his left, clockwise. The right hand represented his jeering *alter ego*. The left hand was the didactic and rational voice. The left hand was able to keep the coin in a glittering spin for much longer than the right.

'You ambidextrous?'

'Yes, always was.'

70

The Irishman watched the boy's frowning, teeth clenched concentration for a while, then removed the untouched beer and poured him a double whisky. 'You drink that and get on the train and sleep.'

'Thanks, Mike. Thanks.'

'That was a nice girl you had with you last time.'

'I've quarrelled with her. Or rather, she's given me the boot. And quite right, too.'

After the visit to the doctor Charlie had gone straight to Jenny. He had guyed the interview while she sat, gravely listening. Then he had given her his favourite lecture on the cross and unalterable insensibility of anybody anywhere born middle-class. No one but Jenny ever heard this lecture. She said at last: 'You *should* go and see a psychiatrist. No, don't you see, it's not fair.'

'Who to, me?'

'No, me. What's the use of shouting at me all the time. You should be saying these things to him.'

'*What?*'

'Well, surely you can see that. You spend all your time lecturing me. You make use of me, Charles.' (She always called him Charles.)

What she was really saying was: 'You should be making love to me, not lecturing me.' Charlie did not really like making love to Jenny. He forced himself when her increasingly tart and accusing manner reminded him that he ought to. He had another girl, whom he disliked, a tall crisp middle-class girl called Sally. She called him, mocking: Charlie-boy. When he had slammed out of Jenny's room, he had gone to Sally and fought his way into her bed. Every act of sex with Sally was a slow, cold subjugation of her by him. That night he had said, when she lay at last, submissive,

71

beneath him: 'Horny-handed son of toil wins by his unquenched virility beautiful daughter of the moneyed classes. And doesn't she love it.'

'Oh yes I do, Charlie-boy.'

'I'm nothing but a bloody sex symbol.'

'Well,' she murmured, already self-possessed, freeing herself, 'that's all I am to you.' She added defiantly, showing that she did care, and that it was Charlie's fault: 'And I couldn't care less.'

'Dear Sally, what I like about you is your beautiful honesty.'

'Is that what you like about me? I thought it was the thrill of beating me down.'

Charlie said to the Irishman: 'I've quarrelled with everyone I know in the last weeks.'

'Quarrelled with your family, too?'

'*No*,' he said, appalled, while the room again swung around him. 'Good Lord no,' he said in a different tone – grateful. He added savagely: 'How could I? I can never say anything to them I really think.' He looked at Mike to see if he had actually said these words aloud. He had, because now Mike said: 'So you know how I feel. I've lived thirty years in this mucking country, and if you arrogant sods knew what I'm thinking half the time.'

'Liar. You say whatever you think, from Cromwell to the Black and Tans and Casement. You never let up. But it's not hurting yourself to say it.'

'Yourself, is it?'

'Yes. But it's all insane. Do you realize how insane it all is, Mike? There's my father. Pillar of the working-class. Labour Party, Trade Union, the lot. But I've been watching my tongue not to say I spent last term

72

campaigning about – he takes it for granted even *now* that the British should push the wogs around.'

'You're a great nation,' said the Irishman. 'But it's not your personal fault, so drink up and have another.'

Charlie drank his first Scotch, and drew the second glass towards him. 'Don't you see what I mean?' he said, his voice rising excitedly. 'Don't you see that it's all *insane*? There's my mother, her sister is ill and it looks as if she'll die. There are two kids, and my mother'll take them both. They're nippers, three and four, it's like starting a family all over again. She thinks nothing of it. If someone's in trouble, she's the mug, every time. But there she sits and says: Those juvenile offenders ought to be flogged until they are senseless. She read it in the papers and so she says it. She said it to me and I kept my mouth shut. And they're all alike.'

'Yes, but you're not going to change it, Charlie, so drink up.'

A man standing a few feet down the bar had a paper sticking out of his pocket. Mike said to him: 'Mind if I borrow your paper for the winners, sir?'

'Help yourself.'

Mike turned the paper over to the back page. 'I had five quid on today,' he said. 'Lost it. Lovely bit of horse-flesh, but I lost it.'

'Wait,' said Charlie excitedly, straightening the paper so he could see the front page. WARDROBE MURDERER GETS SECOND CHANCE, it said. 'See that?' said Charlie. 'The Home Secretary says he can have another chance, they can review the case, he says.'

The Irishman read, cold-faced. 'So he does,' he said.

'Well, I mean to say, there's some decency left, then, I mean if the case can be reviewed it shows they do *care* about something at least.'

'I don't see it your way at all. It's England *versus* England, that's all. Fair play all round, but they'll hang the poor sod on the day appointed as usual.' He turned the newspaper and studied the race news.

Charlie waited for his eyes to clear, held himself steady with one hand flat on the counter, and drank his second double. He pushed over a pound note, remembering it had to last three days, and that now he had quarrelled with Jenny there was no place for him to stay in London.

'No, it's on me,' said Mike. 'I asked you. It's been a pleasure seeing you, Charlie. And don't take the sins of the world on your personal shoulders, lad, because that doesn't do anyone any good, does it now?'

'See you at Christmas, Mike, and thanks.'

He walked carefully out into the rain. There was no solitude to be had on the train that night, so he chose a compartment with one person in it, and settled himself in a corner before looking to see who it was he had with him. It was a girl. He saw then that she was pretty, and then that she was upper-class. Another Sally, he thought, sensing danger, seeing the cool, self-sufficient little face. Hey, there, Charlie, he said to himself, keep yourself in order, or you've had it. He carefully located himself: *he*, Charlie, was now a warm, whisky-comforted belly, already a little sick. Close above it, like a silent loud-speaker, was the source of the hectoring voice. Behind his shoulder waited his grinning familiar. *He must keep them all apart.* He tested the didactic voice: 'It's not your fault, poor bitch, victim of the class-system, she can't help she sees everyone under her like dirt . . .' But the alcohol was working strongly and meanwhile his familiar was calculating: She's had a good look, but can't make me out. My clothes are

74

right, my haircut's on the line, but there's something that makes her wonder. She's waiting for me to speak, then she'll make up her mind. Well, first I'll get her, and then I'll speak.

He caught her eyes and signalled an invitation, but it was an aggressive invitation, to make it as hard for her as he could. After a bit, she smiled at him. Then he roughened his speech to the point of unintelligibility and said: ''Appen you'd like t'window up? What wi' t'rain and t'wind and all.'

'What?' she said sharply, her face lengthening into such a comical frankness of shock that he laughed out, and afterwards inquired impeccably: 'Actually it is rather cold, isn't it? Wouldn't you like to have the window up?' She picked up a magazine and shut him out, while he watched, grinning, the blood creep up from her neat suit collar to her hair-line.

The door slid back; two people came in. They were a man and his wife, both small, crumpled in face and flesh, and dressed in their best for London. There was a fuss and a heaving of suitcases and murmured apologies because of the two superior young people. Then the woman, having settled herself in a corner, looked steadily at Charlie, while he thought: Deep calls to deep, *she* knows who I am all right, she's not foxed by the trimmings. He was right, because soon she said familiarly: 'Would you put the window up for me, lad? It's a rare cold night and no mistake.'

Charlie put up the window, not looking at the girl, who was hiding behind the magazine. Now the woman smiled, and the man smiled, too, because of her ease with the youth.

'You comfortable like that, Father?' she asked.

'Fair enough,' said the husband on the stoical note of the confirmed grumbler.

'Put your feet up beside me, any road.'

'But I'm all right, lass,' he said bravely. Then, making a favour of it, he loosened his laces, eased his feet inside too-new shoes, and set them on the seat beside his wife.

She, for her part, was removing her hat. It was of shapeless grey felt, with a pink rose at the front. Charlie's mother owned just such a badge of respectability, renewed every year or so at the sales. Hers was always bluish felt, with a bit of ribbon or coarse net, and she would rather be seen dead than without it in public.

The woman sat fingering her hair, which was thin and greying. For some reason, the sight of her clean pinkish scalp shining through the grey wisps made Charlie wild with anger. He was taken by surprise, and again summoned himself to himself, making the didactic voice lecture: 'The working woman of these islands enjoys a position in the family superior to that of the middle-class woman, etc., etc., etc.' This was an article he had read recently, and he continued to recite from it, until he realized the voice had become an open sneer, and was saying: 'Not only is she the emotional bulwark of the family, but she is frequently the breadwinner as well, such as wrapping sweets at night, sweated labour for pleasure, anything to get out of the happy home for a few hours.'

The fusion of the two voices, the nagging inside voice, and the jeer from the dangerous force outside, terrified Charlie, and he told himself hastily: 'You're drunk, that's all, now keep your mouth shut, for God's sake.'

The woman was asking him: 'Are you feeling all right?'

'Yes, I'm all right,' he said carefully.

'Going all the way to London?'

'Yes, I'm going all the way to London.'

'It's a long drag.'

'Yes, it's a long drag.'

At this echoing dialogue, the girl lowered her magazine to give him a sharp contemptuous look, up and down. Her face was now smoothly pink, and her small pink mouth was judging.

'You have a mouth like a rosebud,' said Charlie, listening horrified to these words emerging from him.

The girl jerked up the magazine. The man looked sharply at Charlie, to see if he had heard aright, and then at his wife, for guidance. The wife looked doubtfully at Charlie, who offered her a slow desperate wink. She accepted it, and nodded at her husband: boys will be boys. They both glanced warily at the shining face of the magazine.

'We're on our way to London, too,' said the woman.

'So you're on your way to London.'

Stop it, he told himself. He felt a foolish slack grin on his face, and his tongue was thickening in his mouth. He shut his eyes, trying to summon Charlie to his aid, but his stomach was rolling, warm and sick. He lit a cigarette for support, watching his hands at work. 'Lily-handed son of learning wants a manicure badly,' commented a soft voice in his ear; and he saw the cigarette droop in a parody of a cad's gesture between displayed nicotined fingers. Charlie, smoking with poise, sat preserving a polite, sarcastic smile.

He was in the grip of terror. He was afraid he might slide off the seat. He could no longer help himself.

'London's a big place, for strangers,' said the woman.

'But it makes a nice change,' said Charlie, trying hard.

The woman, delighted that a real conversation was at last under way, settled her shabby old head against a leather bulge, and said: 'Yes, it does make a nice change.' The shine on the leather confused Charlie's eyes; he glanced over at the magazine, but its glitter, too, seemed to invade his pupils. He looked at the dirty floor for comfort, and said: 'It's good for people to get a change now and then.'

'Yes, that's what I tell my husband, don't I, Father? It's good for us to get away now and then. We have a married daughter in Streatham.'

'It's a great thing, family ties.'

'Yes, but it's a drag,' said the man. 'Say what you like, but it is. After all, I mean, when all is said and done.' He paused, his head on one side, with a debating look, waiting for Charlie to take it up.

Charlie said: 'There's no denying it, say what you like, I mean, there's no doubt about *that*.' And he looked interestedly at the man for his reply.

The woman said: 'Yes, but the way I look at it, you've got to get *out* of yourself sometimes, look at it that way.'

'It's all very well,' said the husband, on a satisfied but grumbling note, 'but if you're going to do that, well, for a start-off, it's an expense.'

'If you don't throw a good penny after a bad one,' said Charlie judiciously, 'I mean, what's the point.'

'Yes, that's it,' said the woman excitedly, her old face animated. 'That's what I say to Father, what's the point if you don't sometimes let yourself go?'

'I mean, life's bad enough as it is,' said Charlie,

watching the magazine slowly lower itself. It was laid precisely on the seat. The girl now sat, two small brown-gloved hands in a ginger-tweeded lap, staring him out. Her blue eyes glinted into his, and he looked quickly away.

'Well, I can see that right enough,' said the man, 'but there again, you've got to know where to stop.'

'That's right,' said Charlie, 'you're dead right.'

'I know it's all right for some,' said the man, 'I know that, but if you're going to do that, you've got to consider, that's what I think.'

'But, Father, you know you enjoy it, once you're there and Joyce has settled you in your own corner with your own chair and your cup to yourself.'

'Ah,' said the man, nodding heavily, 'but it's not as easy as that now, is it? Well, I mean, that stands to reason.'

'Ah,' said Charlie, shaking his head, feeling it roll heavily in the socket of his neck, 'but if you're going to consider it all, then what's the point? I mean, what I think is, for a start-off, there's no doubt about it.'

The woman hesitated, started to say something, but let her small bright eyes falter away. She was beginning to colour.

Charlie went on compulsively, his head turning like a clockwork-man's – 'It's what you're used to, that's what I say, well I mean. *Well*, and there's another thing, when all is said and done, and after all, if you're going to take one thing with another . . .'

'Stop it,' said the girl, in a sharp, high voice.

'It's a question of principle,' said Charlie, but his head had stopped rolling and his eyes had focused.

'If you don't stop, I'm going to call the guard and have you put in another compartment,' said the girl.

To the old people she said in a righteous scandalized voice: 'Can't you see he's laughing at you? Can't you see?' She lifted the magazine again.

The old people looked suspiciously at Charlie, dubiously at each other. The woman's face was very pink and her eyes bright and hot.

'I think I am going to get forty winks,' said the man, with general hostility. He settled his feet, put his head back, and closed his eyes.

Charlie said: 'Excuse me,' and scrambled his way to the corridor over the legs of the man, then the legs of the woman, muttering 'Excuse me, excuse me, I'm sorry.'

He stood in the corridor, his back jolting slightly against the shifting wood of the compartment's sides. His eyes were shut, his tears running. Words, no longer articulate, muttered and jumbled somewhere inside him, a stream of frightened protesting phrases.

Wood slid against wood close to his ear, and he heard the softness of clothed flesh on wood.

'If it's that bloody little bint, I'll kill her,' said a voice, small and quiet, from his diaphragm.

He opened his murderous eyes on the woman. She looked concerned.

'I'm sorry,' he said, stiff and sullen, 'I'm sorry, I didn't mean . . .'

'It's all right,' she said, and laid her two red hands on his crossed quivering forearms. She took his two wrists, and laid his arms gently down by his sides. 'Don't take on,' she said, 'it's all right, it's all right, son.'

The tense rejection of his flesh caused her to take a step back from him. But there she stood her ground and said: 'Now look, son, there's no point taking on

80

like that, well, is there? I mean to say, you've got to take the rough with the smooth, and there's no other way of looking at it.'

She waited, facing him, troubled but sure of herself.

After a while Charlie said: 'Yes, I suppose you're right.'

She nodded and smiled, and went back into the compartment. After a moment, Charlie followed her.

NOTES FOR A CASE HISTORY

Maureen Watson was born at 93 Nelson's Way, N1, in 1942. She did not remember the war. Or rather, when people said 'The War', she thought of Austerity: couponed curtains, traded clothes, the half-pound of butter swapped for the quarter of tea. (Maureen's parents preferred tea to butter.) Farther back, at the roots of her life, she *felt* a movement of fire and shadow, a leaping and a subsidence of light. She did not know whether this was a memory of a picture she had formed, perhaps from what her parents had told her of the night the bomb fell two streets from Nelson's Way and they had all stood among piles of smoking rubble for a day and night, watching firemen hose the flames. This feeling was not only of danger, but of fatality, of being helpless before great impersonal forces; and was how she most deeply felt, saw, or thought an early childhood which the social viewer would describe perhaps like this: 'Maureen Watson, conceived by chance on an unexpected granted-at-the-last-minute leave, at the height of the worst war in history, infant support of a mother only occasionally upheld (the chances of war deciding) by a husband she had met in a bomb shelter during an air-raid; poor baby, born into a historical upheaval which destroyed forty million people and might very well have destroyed her.'

As for Maureen, her memories and the reminiscences of her parents made her dismiss the whole business as boring, and nothing to do with her.

It was at her seventh birthday party she first made this clear. She wore a mauve organdie frock with a pink sash, and her golden hair was in ringlets. One of the mothers said: 'This is the first unrationed party dress my Shirley has had. It's a shame, isn't it?' and her own mother said: 'Well, of course these war children don't know what they've missed.' At which Maureen said: '*I* am not a war child.' 'What are you then, love?' said her mother, fondly exchanging glances. 'I'm Maureen,' said Maureen.

'And I'm Shirley,' said Shirley, joining cause.

Shirley Banner was Maureen's best friend. The Watsons and the Banners were better than the rest of the street. The Watsons lived in an end house, at higher weekly payments. The Banners had a sweets-paper-and-tobacco shop.

Maureen and Shirley remembered (or had they been told?) that once Nelson's Way was a curved terrace of houses. Then the ground floor level had broken into shops: a grocer's, a laundry, a hardware, a baker, a dairy. It seemed as if every second family in the street ran a shop to supply certain defined needs of the other families. What other needs were there? Apparently none; for Maureen's parents applied for permission to the Council, and the ground floor of their house became a second grocery shop, by way of broken-down walls, new shelves, a deep-freeze. Maureen remembered two small rooms, each with flowered curtains where deep shadows moved and flickered from the two small fires that burned back-to-back in the centre wall that divided them. These two rooms disappeared in clouds of dust from which sweet-smelling planks of wood stuck out. Strange, but friendly, men paid her compliments on her golden corkscrews and asked her for kisses, which they certainly did not get. They gave her sips of sweet tea from their canteens (filled twice a day by her mother) and made her bracelets of the spiralling fringes of yellow wood. Then they disappeared. There was the new shop. Maureen's Shop. Maureen went with her mother to the sign-shop to arrange for these two words to be written in yellow paint on a blue ground.

Even without the name Maureen would have known that the shop was connected with hopes for her future; and that her future was what her mother lived for.

She was pretty. She had always known it. Even where the shadows of fire and dark were, they had played over a pretty baby. 'You were such a pretty baby, Maureen.' And at the birthday parties: 'Maureen's growing really pretty, Mrs Watson.' But all babies and little girls are pretty, she knew that well enough . . . no, it was something more. For Shirley was plump, dark – pretty. Yet their parents', or rather, their mother's talk, had made it clear from the start that Shirley was not in the same class as Maureen.

When Maureen was ten there was an episode of importance. The two mothers were in the room above Maureen's Shop and they were brushing their little girls' hair out. Shirley's mother said: 'Maureen could do really well for herself, Mrs Watson.' And Mrs Watson nodded, but sighed deeply. The sigh annoyed Maureen, because it contradicted the absolute certainty that she felt (it had been bred into her) about her future. Also because it had to do with the *boring* era which she remembered, or thought she did, as a tiger-striped movement of fire. *Chance*: Mrs Watson's sigh was like a prayer to the Gods of Luck: it was the sigh of a small helpless thing being tossed about by big seas and gales. Maureen made a decision, there and then, that she had nothing in common with the little people who were prepared to be helpless and tossed about. For she was going to be quite different. She was already different. Not only the War, but the shadows of war had long gone, except for talk in the newspapers which had nothing to do with her. The shops were full of everything. The Banners' sweets-tobacco-paper shop had just been done up; and *Maureen's* was short of nothing. Maureen and Shirley, two pretty little girls in smart mother-made dresses were children of plenty, and knew it, because their parents kept saying (apparently they did not care how tedious they were) 'These kids don't lack for anything, do they, they don't know what it can be like, do they?' This, with the suggestion that they ought to be grateful for not lacking anything, always made the children sulky, and they went off to flirt their full many-petticoated skirts where the neighbours could see them and pay them compliments.

Eleven years. Twelve years. Already Shirley had subsided into her rôle of pretty girl's plainer girl-friend, although, of course, she was not plain at all. Fair girl, dark girl, and Maureen by mysterious birthright was the 'pretty one', and there was no doubt in either of their minds which girl the boys would try first for a date. Yet this balance was by no means as unfair as it seemed. Maureen, parrying and jesting on street-corners, at bus stops, knew she was doing battle for two, because the boys she discarded, Shirley got: Shirley got far more boys than she would have done without

Maureen who, for her part, needed, more – *had* to have a foil. Her rôle demanded one.

They both left school at fifteen, Maureen to work in the shop. She was keeping her eyes open: her mother's phrase. She wore a slim white overall, pinned her fair curls up, was neat and pretty in her movements. She smiled calmly when customers said: 'My word, Mrs Watson, your Maureen's turned out, hasn't she?'

About that time there was a second moment of consciousness. Mrs Watson was finishing a new dress for Maureen, and the fitting was taking rather long. Maureen fidgeted and her mother said: 'Well, it's your capital, isn't it? You've got to see that, love.' And she added the deep unconscious sigh. Maureen said: 'Well, don't go on about it, it's not very nice, is it?' And what she meant was, not that the idea was not very nice, but that she had gone beyond needing to be reminded about it; she was feeling the irritated embarrassment of a child when it is reminded to clean its teeth after this habit has become second nature. Mrs Watson saw and understood this, and sighed again; and this time it was the maternal sigh which means: Oh dear, you are growing up fast! 'Oh, *mum*,' said Maureen, 'sometimes you just make me tired, you do really.'

Sixteen. She was managing her capital perfectly. Her assets were a slight delicate prettiness, and a dress sense that must have been a gift from God, or more probably because she had been reading the fashion magazines since practically before consciousness. Shirley had put in six months of beehive hair, pouting scarlet lips, and an air of sullen disdain; but Maureen's sense of herself was much finer. She modelled herself on film-stars, but with an understanding of how far she could go – of what was allowable to Maureen. So the experience of being Bardot, Monroe, or whoever it was, refined her: she took from it an essence, which was learning to be a vehicle for other people's fantasies. So while Shirley had been a dozen stars, but really *been* them, in violent temporary transmogrifications, from which she emerged (often enough with a laugh) Shirley – plump, good-natured, and herself; Maureen remained herself through every rôle, but creating her appearance, like an *alter ego*, to meet the expression in people's eyes.

Round about sixteen, another incident: prophetic. Mrs Watson had a cousin who worked in the dress-trade, and this man, unthought-of for many years, was met at a wedding. He commented on Maureen, a vision in white gauze. Mrs Watson worked secretly on this slender material for some weeks; then wrote to him: could Maureen be a model? He had only remote connections with the world of expensive clothes and girls, but he dropped into the shop with frankly personal aims. Maureen, in a white wrapper, was still pretty, very; but her remote air told this shrewd man that she would certainly not go out with him. She was saving herself; he knew that air of self-esteem very well from other exemplars. Such girls do not go out with middle-aged cousins, except as a favour or to get something. However, he told Mrs Watson that Maureen was definitely model material, but that she would have to do something about her voice. (He meant her accent, of course; and so Mrs Watson understood him.) He left addresses and advice, and Mrs Watson was in a state of quivering ambition. She said so to Maureen: 'This is your chance, girl. Take it.' What Maureen heard was: 'This is *my* chance.'

Maureen, nothing if not alert for her Big Chance, for which her whole life had prepared her, accepted her mother's gift of £100 (she did not thank her, no thanks were due) and actually wrote to the school where she would be taught Voice Training.

Then she fell into sullen withdrawal, which she understood so little that a week had gone by before she said she must be sick – or something. She was rude to her mother: very rare, this. Her father chided her for it: even rarer. But he spoke in such a way that Maureen understood for the first time that this drive, this push, this family effort to gain her a glamorous future came from her mother, her father was not implicated. For him, she was a pretty enough girl, spoiled by a silly woman.

Maureen slowly understood she was not sick, she was growing up. For one thing: if she changed her 'voice' so as to be good enough to mix with new people, she would no longer be part of this street, she would no longer be *our Maureen*. What would she be, then? Her mother knew: she would marry a duke and be whisked off to Hollywood. Maureen examined her mother's ideas for her and shrank with humiliation. She was, above all, no fool, but she had been very foolish. For one thing: when she used her eyes, with the scales of illusion off them, she saw that the million streets of London blossomed with girls as pretty as she. What then had fed the illusion in herself and in other people? What accounted for the special tone, the special looks that always greeted her? Why, nothing more than that she, Maureen, because of her mother's will behind her, had carried herself from childhood as something special, apart, destined for a great future.

Meanwhile (as she clearly saw) she was in 93 Nelson's Way, serving behind the counter of Maureen's Shop. (She now wondered what the neighbours had thought

– before they got used to it – about her mother's fondness so terribly displayed.) She was dependent on nothing less than that a duke or a film producer would walk in to buy a quarter of tea and some sliced bread.

Maureen sulked. So her father said. So her mother complained. Maureen was – thinking? Yes. But more, a wrong had been done her, she knew it, and the sulking was more of a protective silence while she grew a scab over a wound.

She emerged demanding that the £100 should be spent on sending her to Secretarial School. Her parents complained that she could have learned how to be a secretary for nothing if she had stayed on at school another year. She said: 'Yes, but you didn't have the sense to make me, did you? What did you think, I was going to sell butter like you all my life?' Unfair, on the face of it; but deeply fair, in view of what they had done to her. In their different ways they knew it. (Mr Watson knew in his heart, for instance, that he should never have allowed his wife to call the shop 'Maureen's'.) Maureen went, then, to Secretarial School for a year. Shirley went with her: she had been selling cosmetics in the local branch of a big chain-store. To raise the £100 was difficult for Shirley's parents: the shop had done badly, had been bought by a big firm; her father was an assistant in it. For that matter, it wasn't all that easy for the Watsons: the £100 was the result of small savings and pinchings over years.

This was the first time Maureen had thought of the word capital in connection with money, rather than her own natural assets: it was comparatively easy for the Watsons to raise money, because they had capital: the Banners had no capital. (Mrs Watson said the Banners had had *bad luck*.) Maureen strengthened her will; and as a result the two families behaved even more as if the girls would have different futures – or, to put it another way, that while the two sums of a hundred pounds were the same, the Watsons could be expected to earn more on theirs than the Banners.

This was reflected directly in the two girls' discussions about boys.

Shirley would say: 'I'm more easy-going than you.'

Maureen would reply: '*I* only let them go so far.'

Their first decisions on this almighty subject had taken place years before, when they were thirteen. Even then Shirley went further ('let them go further') than Maureen. It was put down, between them, to Shirley's warmer temperament – charitably; for both knew it was because of Maureen's higher value in the market.

At the Secretarial School they met boys they had not met before. Previously boys had been from the street or the neighbourhood, known from birth, and for this reason not often gone out with – that would have been boring. (Serious, with possibilities of marriage.) Or boys picked up after dances or at the pictures. But now there were new boys met day after day in the School. Shirley went out with one for weeks, thought of getting engaged, changed her mind, went out with another. Maureen went out with a dozen, chosen carefully. She knew what she was doing – and scolded Shirley for being so *soft*. 'You're just stupid, Shirl – I mean, you've got to get on, why don't you do like me?'

What Maureen did was to allow herself to be courted, until she agreed at last, as a favour, to be taken out. First, lunch – a word she began to use now. She would agree to go out to lunch two or three times with one boy, while she was taken out to supper (dinner) by another. The dinner partner, having been rewarded by

90

a closed-mouth kiss for eight, ten, twelve nights, got angry or sulky or reproachful, according to his nature. He dropped her, and the lunch partner was promoted to dinner partner.

Maureen ate free for the year of her training. It wasn't that she planned it like this: but when she heard other girls say they paid their way or liked to be independent, it seemed to Maureen wrong-headed. To pay for herself would be to let herself be undervalued: even the idea of it made her nervous and even sulky.

At the end of the training Maureen got a job in a big architects' office. She was a junior typist. She stuck out for a professional office because the whole point of the training was to enable her to meet a better class of people. Of course she had already learned not to use the phrase, and when her mother did snubbed her with: 'I don't know what you mean, better *class*, but it's not much point my going into that hardware stuck upstairs in an office by myself if I can get a job where there's some life about.'

Shirley went into a draper's shop where there was one other typist (female) and five male assistants.

In Maureen's place there were six architects, out most of the time, or invisible in large offices visited only by the real secretaries; a lower stratum of young men in training, designers, draftsmen, managers, etc.; and a pool of typists.

The young men were mostly of her own class. For some months she ate and was entertained at their expense; and at each week-end there was a solemn ceremony, the highpoint of the week, certainly the most exciting moment in it, when she divided her wage. It was seven pounds (rising to ten in three years) and she allocated two pounds for clothes, four for the post office, and one pound for the week's odd expenses.

At the end of a year she understood two things. That she had saved something like £200. That there was not a young man in the office who would take her out again. They regarded her, according to their natures, with resentment or with admiration for her cool management of them. But there was nothing doing *there* – so they all knew.

Maureen thought this over. If she were not taken out to meals and entertainment, she must pay for herself and save no money, or she must never go out at all. If she was going to be taken out, then she must give something in return. What she gave was an open mouth, and freedom to the waist. She calculated that because of her prettiness she could give much less than other girls.

She was using her *capital* with even more intelligence than before. A good part of her time – all not spent in the office or being taken out, went in front of her looking-glass, or with the better-class fashion magazines. She studied them with formidable concentration. By now she knew she could have gone anywhere in these islands, except for her voice. Whereas, months before, she had sulked in a sort of fright at the idea of cutting herself off from her street and the neighbours, now she softened and shaped her voice, listening to the clients and the senior architects in the office. She knew her voice had changed when Shirley said: 'You're talking nice, Maureen, much nicer than me.'

There was a boy in the office who teased her about it. His name was Tony Head. He was in training to be an accountant for the firm, and was very much from her own background. After having taken her out twice to lunch, he had never asked her again. She knew why:

he had told her. 'Can't afford you, Maureen,' he said. He earned not much more than she did. He was nineteen, ambitious, serious, and she liked him.

Then she was nineteen. Shirley was engaged to one of the assistants in her shop, and would be married next Christmas.

Maureen took forty pounds out of her savings and went on a tour to Italy. It was her first time out of England. She hated it: not Italy, but the fact that half the sixty people on the tour were girls, like herself, looking for a good time, and the other half elderly couples. In Rome, Pisa, Florence, Venice, the Italians mooned over Maureen, courted her with melting eyes, while she walked past them, distant as a starlet. They probably thought she was one. The courier, a sharp young man, took Maureen out to supper one night after he had finished his duties, and made it clear that her mouth, even if opened, and her breasts, were not enough. Maureen smiled at him sweetly through the rest of the trip. No one paid her odd coffees, ices, and drinks. On the last night of the trip, in a panic because the £40 investment had yielded so little, she went out with an Italian boy who spoke seven words of English. She thought him crude, and left him after an hour.

But she had learned a good deal for her forty pounds. Quietly, in her lunch-hour, she went off to the National Gallery and to the Tate. There she looked, critical and respectful, at pictures, memorizing their subjects, or main colours, learning names. When invited out, she asked to be taken to 'foreign' films, and when she got back home wrote down the names of the director and the stars. She looked at the book page of the *Express* (she made her parents buy it instead of the *Mirror*) and

93

sometimes bought a recommended book, if it was a best-seller.

Twenty. Shirley was married and had a baby. Maureen saw little of her – both girls felt they had a new world of knowledge the other couldn't appreciate.

Maureen was earning £10 a week, and saved six.

There came to the office as an apprentice architect, Stanley Hunt, from grammar school and technical college. Tallish, well-dressed, fair with a small moustache. They took each other's measure, knowing they were the same kind. It was some weeks before he asked her out. She knew, by putting herself in his place, that he was looking for a wife with a little money or a house of her own, if he couldn't get a lady. (She smiled when she heard him using this word about one of the clients.) He tried to know clients socially, to be accepted by them as they accepted the senior architects. All this Maureen watched, her cool little face saying nothing.

One day, after he had invited a Miss Plast (Chelsea, well-off, investing money in houses) to coffee, and been turned down, he asked Maureen to join him in a sandwich lunch. Maureen thanked him delightfully, but said she already had an engagement. She went off to the National Gallery, sat on the steps, froze off wolves and pick-ups, and ate a sandwich by herself.

A week later, invited to lunch by Stanley, she suggested the Trattoria Siciliana which was more expensive, as she knew quite well, than he had expected. But this meal was a success. He was impressed with her, though he knew (how could he not, when his was similar?) her background.

She was careful to be engaged for two weeks. Then she agreed to go to the pictures – 'a foreign film, if you don't mind, I think the American films are just boring.'

She did not offer to pay, but remarked casually that she had nearly six hundred pounds in the post office. 'I'm thinking of buying a little business, some time. A dress shop. I've got a cousin in the trade.'

Stanley agreed that 'with your taste' it would be sure a thing.

Maureen no longer went to the Palais, or similar places (though she certainly did not conceal from Stanley that she had 'once') but she loved to dance. Twice they went to the West End together and danced at a Club which was 'a nice place'. They danced well together. On the second occasion she offered to pay her share, for the first time in her life. He refused, as she had known he would, but she could see he liked her for offering: more, was relieved; in the office they said she was mean, and he must have heard them. On that night, taken home lingeringly, she opened her mouth for him and let his hands go down to her thighs. She felt a sharp sexuality which made her congratulate herself that she had never, like Shirley, gone 'half-way' before. Well, of course girls were going to get married to just anybody if they let themselves be all worked up every time they were taken out!

But Stanley was not at all caught. He was too cool a customer, as she was. He was still looking for something better.

He would be an architect in a couple of years; he would be in a profession; he was putting down money for a house; he was good-looking, attractive to women, and with these assets he ought to do better than marry Maureen. Maureen agreed with him.

But meanwhile, he took her out. She was careful often to be engaged elsewhere. She was careful always to be worth taking somewhere expensive. When he took her home, while she did not go so far as 'nearly the whole way', she went 'everything but'; and she was glad she did not like him better, because otherwise she would have been lost. She knew quite well she did not really like him, although her mind was clouded by her response to his hands, his moustache, his clothes and his new car.

She knew, because meanwhile a relationship she understood very well, and regretted, had grown up with Tony. He, watching this duel between the well-matched pair, would grin and drop remarks at which Maureen coloured and turned coldly away. He often asked her out – but only for 'a Dutch treat' – expecting her to refuse. 'How's your savings account, Maureen? I can't save, you girls get it all spent on you.' Tony took out a good many girls: Maureen kept a count of them. She hated him; yet she liked him, and knew she did. She relied on him above all for this grinning, honest understanding of her: he did not approve of her, but perhaps (she felt in her heart) he was right? During this period she several times burst into tears when alone, without apparent reason; afterwards she felt that life had no flavour. Her future was narrowing down to Stanley; and at these times she viewed it through Tony Head's eyes.

One night the firm had a party for the senior members of the staff. Stanley was senior, Maureen and Tony were not. Maureen knew that Stanley had previously asked another girl to go, and when he asked herself, was uncertain whether she could make it until the very last moment; particularly as his inviting her, a junior, meant that he was trying out on the senior members the idea of Maureen as a wife. But she acquitted herself very well. First, she was the best-looking woman in the room by far, and the best-dressed. Everyone looked at her and commented: they were used to her as a pretty typist; but tonight she was using all her will to make them look at her, to make her face and body reflect what they admired. She made no mistakes. When the party was over Stanley and two of the younger architects suggested they drive out to London airport for breakfast, and they did. The two other girls were middle class. Maureen kept silent for the most part, smiling serenely. She had been to Italy, she remarked, when a plane rose to go to Italy. Yes, she had liked it, though she thought the Italians were too noisy; what she had enjoyed best was the Sistine Chapel and a boat trip on the Adriatic. She hadn't cared for Venice much, it was beautiful, but the canals smelled, and there were far too many people: perhaps it would be better to go in winter? She said all this, having a right to it, and it came off. As she spoke she remembered Tony, who had once met her on her way to the National Gallery: 'Getting yourself an education, Maureen? That's right, it'll pay off well, that will.'

She knew, thinking it all over afterwards, that the evening had been important for her with Stanley. Because of this, she did not go out with him for a week, she said she was busy talking to her cousin about the possibilities of a dress-shop. She sat in her room thinking about Stanley, and when thoughts of Tony came into her mind, irritatedly pushed them away. If she could succeed with Stanley, why not with someone better? The two architects from that evening had eyed her all the following week: they did not, however, ask her out. She then found that both were engaged to marry the girls they had been with. It was bad luck: she was sure that otherwise they would have asked her out. How to meet more like them? Well, that was the trouble – the drive to the airport was a bit of a fluke; it was the first time she had actually met the seniors socially.

Meanwhile, Stanley showed an impatience in his courtship – and for the first time. As for her, she was getting on for twenty-two, and all the girls she had grown up with were married and had their first or even their second babies.

She went out with Stanley to a dinner in the West End at an Italian restaurant. Afterwards they were both very passionate. Maureen, afterwards, was furious with herself: some borderline had been crossed (she supposed she still could be called a virgin?) and now decisions would have to be made.

Stanley was in love with her. She was in love with Stanley. A week later he proposed to her. It was done with a violent moaning intensity that she knew was due to his conflicts over marrying her. She was not good enough. He was not good enough. They were second-best for each other. They writhed and moaned and bit in the car, and agreed to marry. Her eight hundred pounds would make it easier to buy the house in a good suburb. He would formally meet her parents next Sunday.

'So you're engaged to Stanley Hunt?' said Tony.

'Looks like it, doesn't it?'

'Caught him – good for you!'

'He's caught me, more like it!'

'Have it your way.'

She was red and angry. He was serious.

'Come and have a bite?' he said. She went.

It was a small restaurant, full of office workers eating on luncheon vouchers. She ate fried plaice (no chips,

98

please) and he ate steak-and-kidney pudding. He joked, watched her, watched her intently, said finally: 'Can't you do better than that?' He meant, and she knew it, better in the sense she would use herself, in her heart: he meant *nice*. Like himself. But did that mean that Tony thought *she* was nice? Unlike Stanley? She did not think she was, she was moved to tears (concealed) that he did. 'What's wrong with him, then?' she demanded, casual. 'What's wrong with *you* – you need your head examined.' He said it seriously, and they exchanged a long look. The two of them sat looking good-bye at each other: the extremely pretty girl at whom everyone in the room kept glancing and remarking on, and the good-looking, dark, rather fat young accountant who was brusque and solemn with disappointment in her. With love for her? Very likely.

She went home silent, thinking of Tony. When she thought of him she needed to cry. She also needed to hurt him.

But she told her parents she was engaged to Stanley, who would be an architect. They would have their own house, in (they thought) Hemel Hempstead. He owned a car. He was coming to tea on Sunday. Her mother forgot the dukes and the film producers before the announcement ended: her father listened judiciously, then congratulated her. He had been going to a football match on Sunday, but agreed, after persuasion, that this was a good enough reason to stay home.

Her mother then began discussing, with deference to Maureen's superior knowledge, how to manage next Sunday to best advantage. For four days she went on about it. But she was talking to herself. Her husband listened, said nothing. And Maureen listened, critically, like her father. Mrs Watson began clamouring for a definite opinion on what sort of cake to serve on Sunday. But Maureen had no opinion. She sat, quiet, looking at her mother, a largish ageing woman, her ex-fair hair dyed yellow, her flesh guttering. She was like an excited child, and it was not attractive. *Stupid, stupid, stupid* – that's all you are, thought Maureen.

As for Maureen, if anyone had made the comparison, she was 'sulking' as she had before over being a model and having to be drilled out of her 'voice'. She said nothing but: 'It'll be all right, mum, don't get so worked up.' Which was true, because Stanley knew what to expect: he knew why he had not been invited to meet her parents until properly hooked. He would have done the same in her place. He *was* doing the same: she was going to meet his parents the week after. What Mrs Watson, Mr Watson, wore on Sunday; whether sandwiches or cake were served; whether there were fresh or artificial flowers – none of it mattered. The Watsons were part of the bargain: what he was paying in return for publicly owning the most covetable woman anywhere they were likely to be; and for the right to sleep with her after the public display.

Meanwhile, Maureen said not a word. She sat on her bed looking at nothing in particular. Once or twice she examined her face in the mirror, and even put cream on it. And she cut out a dress, but put it aside.

On Sunday Mrs Watson laid tea for four, using her own judgement since Maureen was too deeply in love (so she told everyone) to notice such trifles. At four Stanley was expected, and at 3.55 Maureen descended to the living-room. She wore: a faded pink dress from three summers before; her mother's cretonne overall used for housework; and a piece of cloth tied round her hair that might very well have been a duster. At any rate, it was a faded grey. She had put on a pair of her mother's old shoes. She could not be called plain; but she looked like her own faded elder sister, dressed for a hard day's spring-cleaning.

Her father, knowledgeable, said nothing: he lowered the paper, examined her, let out a short laugh, and lifted it again. Mrs Watson, understanding at last that this was a real crisis, burst into tears. Stanley arrived before Mrs Watson could stop herself crying. He nearly said to Mrs Watson: I didn't know Maureen had an older sister. Maureen sat listless at one end of the table; Mr Watson sat grinning at the other, and Mrs Watson sniffed and wiped her eyes between the two.

Maureen said: 'Hello, Stanley, meet my father and mother.' He shook their hands and stared at her. She did not meet his eyes: rather, the surface of her blue gaze met the furious, incredulous, hurt pounce of his glares at her. Maureen poured tea, offered him sandwiches and cake, and made conversation about the weather, and the prices of food, and the dangers of giving even good customers credit in the shop. He sat there, a well set-up young man, with his brushed hair, his brushed moustache, his checked brown cloth jacket, and a face flaming with anger and affront. He said nothing, but Maureen talked on, her voice trailing and cool. At five o'clock, Mrs Watson again burst into tears, her whole body shaking, and Stanley brusquely left.

Mr Watson said: 'Well, why did you lead him on, then?' and turned on the television. Mrs Watson went to lie down. Maureen, in her own room, took off the various items of her disguise, and returned them to her mother's room. 'Don't cry, mum, what are you carrying on like that for? What's the matter?' Then she dressed extremely carefully in a new white linen suit, brown shoes, beige blouse. She did her hair and her face, and sat looking at herself. The last two hours (or week) hit her, and her stomach hurt so that she doubled up. She cried; but the tears smeared her make-up, and she stopped herself with the side of a fist against her mouth.

It now seemed to her that for the last week she had simply not been Maureen; she had been someone else. What had she done it for? Why? Then she knew it was for Tony: during all that ridiculous scene at the tea-table, she had imagined Tony looking on, grinning, but understanding her.

She now wiped her face quite clear of tears, and went quietly out of the house so as not to disturb her father and mother. There was a telephone booth at the corner. She stepped calm and aloof along the street, her mouth held (as it always was) in an almost-smile. Bert from the grocer's shop said: 'Hey, Maureen, that's a smasher, who's it for?' And she gave him the smile and the toss of the head that went with the street and said: 'You, Bert, it's all for you.' She went to the telephone booth thinking of Tony. She felt as if he already knew what had happened. She would say: 'Let's go and dance, Tony.' He would say: 'Where shall I meet you?' she dialled his number, and it rang and it rang and it rang. She stood holding the receiver, waiting. About ten minutes – more. Slowly she replaced it. *He had let her down.* He had been telling her, in words and without, to be something, to stay something, and now he did not care, he had let her down.

Maureen quietened herself and telephoned Stanley.

Stanley answered, and she said amiably: 'Hello.'

Silence. She could hear him breathing, fast. She could see his affronted face.

'Well, aren't you going to say anything?' She tried

to make this casual, but she could hear the fear in her voice. Oh yes, she could lose him and probably had. To hide the fear she said: 'Can't you take a joke, Stanley?' and laughed.

'A joke!'

She laughed. Not bad, it sounded all right.

'I thought you'd gone off your nut, clean off your rocker . . .' He was breathing in and out, a rasping noise. She was reminded of his hot breathing down her neck and her arms. Her own breath quickened, even while she thought: I don't like him, I really don't like him at all . . . and she said softly: 'Oh, Stan, I was having a bit of giggle, that's all.'

Silence. Now, this was the crucial moment.

'Oh, Stan, can't you see – I thought it was all just boring, that's all it was.' She laughed again.

He said: 'Nice for your parents, I don't think.'

'Oh, they don't mind – they laughed after you'd left, though first they were cross.' She added hastily, afraid he might think they were laughing at him: 'They're used to me, that's all it is.'

Another long silence. With all her will-power she insisted that he should soften. But he said nothing, merely breathed in and out, into the receiver.

'Stanley, it was only a joke, you aren't really angry, are you, Stanley?' The tears sounded in her voice now, and she judged it better that they should.

He said, after hesitation: 'Well, Maureen, I just didn't like it, I don't like that kind of thing, that's all.' She allowed herself to go on crying, and after a while he said, forgiving her in a voice that was condescending and irritated: 'Well, all right, all right, there's no point in crying, is there?'

He was annoyed with himself for giving in, she knew

that, because she would have been. He had given her up, thrown her over, during the last couple of hours: he was pleased, really, that something from outside had forced him to give her up. Now he could be free for the something better that would turn up – someone who would not strike terror into him by an extraordinary performance like this afternoon's.

'Let's go off to the pictures, Stan . . .'

Even now, he hesitated. Then he said, quick and reluctant: 'I'll meet you at Leicester Square, outside the Odeon, at seven o'clock.' He put down the receiver.

Usually he came to pick her up in the car from the corner of the street.

She stood smiling, the tears running down her face. She knew she was crying because of the loss of Tony, who had let her down. She walked back to her house to make up again, thinking that she was in Stanley's power now: there was no balance between them, the advantage was all his.

TO ROOM NINETEEN

This is a story, I suppose, about a failure in intelligence: the Rawlings' marriage was grounded in intelligence.

They were older when they married than most of their married friends: in their well-seasoned late twenties. Both had had a number of affairs, sweet rather than bitter; and when they fell in love – for they did fall in love – had known each other for some time. They joked that they had saved each other 'for the real thing'. That they had waited so long (but not too long) for this real thing was to them a proof of their sensible discrimination. A good many of their friends had married young, and now (they felt) probably regretted lost opportunities; while others, still unmarried, seemed to them arid, self-doubting, and likely to make desperate or romantic marriages.

Not only they, but others, felt they were well-matched: their friends' delight was an additional proof of their happiness. They had played the same rôles, male and female, in this group or set, if such a wide, loosely connected, constantly changing constellation of people could be called a set. They had both become, by virtue of their moderation, their humour, and their abstinence from painful experience, people to whom others came for advice. They could be, and were, relied on. It was one of those cases of a man and a woman linking themselves whom no one else had ever thought of linking, probably because of their similarities. But then everyone exclaimed: Of course! How right! How was it we never thought of it before!

And so they married among general rejoicing, and because of their foresight and their sense for what was probable, nothing was a surprise to them.

Both had well-paid jobs. Matthew was a sub-editor on a large London newspaper, and Susan worked in an advertising firm. He was not the stuff of which editors or publicized journalists are made, but he was much more than 'a sub-editor', being one of the essential background people who in fact steady, inspire and make possible the people in the limelight. He was content with this position. Susan had a talent for commercial drawing. She was humorous about the advertisements she was responsible for, but she did not feel strongly about them one way or the other.

Both, before they had married, had had pleasant flats, but they felt it unwise to base a marriage on either flat, because it might seem like a submission of personality on the part of the one whose flat it was not. They moved into a new flat in South Kensington on the clear understanding that when their marriage had settled down (a process they knew would not take long, and was in fact more humorous concession to popular wisdom than what was due to themselves) they would buy a house and start a family.

And this is what happened. They lived in their charming flat for two years, giving parties and going to them, being a popular young married couple, and then Susan became pregnant, she gave up her job, and they bought a house in Richmond. It was typical of this couple that they had a son first, then a daughter, then twins, son and daughter. Everything right, appropriate, and what everyone would wish for, if they could choose. But people did feel these two had chosen; this balanced and sensible family was no more than what was due to them because of their infallible sense for *choosing* right.

And so they lived with their four children in their gardened house in Richmond and were happy. They had everything they had wanted and had planned for.

And yet . . .

Well, even this was expected that there must be a certain flatness . . .

Yes, yes, of course, it was natural they sometimes felt like this. Like what?

Their life seemed to be like a snake biting its tail. Matthew's job for the sake of Susan, children, house, and garden – which caravanserai needed a well-paid job to maintain it. And Susan's practical intelligence for the sake of Matthew, the children, the house and the garden – which unit would have collapsed in a week without her.

But there was no point about which either could say: 'For the sake of *this* is all the rest.' Children? But children can't be a centre of life and a reason for being. They can be a thousand things that are delightful, interesting, satisfying, but they can't be a well-spring to live from. Or they shouldn't be. Susan and Matthew knew that well enough.

Matthew's job? Ridiculous. It was an interesting job, but scarcely a reason for living. Matthew took pride in doing it well; but he could hardly be expected to be proud of the newspaper: the newspaper he read, *his* newspaper, was not the one he worked for.

Their love for each other? Well, that was nearest it. If this wasn't a centre, what was? Yes, it was around this point, their love, that the whole extraordinary structure revolved. For extraordinary it certainly was. Both Susan and Matthew had moments of thinking so, of looking in secret disbelief at this thing they had created: marriage, four children, big house, garden, charwomen, friends, cars . . . and this *thing*, this entity, all of it had come into existence, been blown into being out of nowhere, because Susan loved Matthew and Matthew loved Susan. Extraordinary. So that was the central point, the well-spring.

And if one felt that it simply was not strong enough, important enough, to support it all, well whose fault was that? Certainly neither Susan's nor Matthew's. It was in the nature of things. And they sensibly blamed neither themselves nor each other.

On the contrary, they used their intelligence to preserve what they had created from a painful and explosive world: they looked around them, and took lessons. All around them, marriages collapsing, or breaking, or rubbing along (even worse, they felt). They must not make the same mistakes, they must not.

They had avoided the pitfall so many of their friends had fallen into – of buying a house in the country *for the sake of the children*; so that the husband became a week-end husband, a week-end father, and the wife always careful not to ask what went on in the town-flat which they called (in joke) a bachelor flat. No, Matthew was a full-time husband, a full-time father, and at nights, in the big married bed in the big married bedroom (which had an attractive view of the river) they lay beside each other talking and he told her about his day, and what he had done, and who he had met; and she told him about her day (not as interesting, but that was not her fault) for both knew of the hidden resentments and deprivations of the woman who has lived her own life and, above all, has earned her own living, and is now dependent on a husband for outside interests and money.

Nor did Susan make the mistake of taking a job for the sake of her independence, which she might very well have done, since her old firm, missing her qualities of humour, balance, and sense, invited her often to go back. Children needed their mother to a certain age, that both parents knew and agreed on; and when these four healthy wisely-brought-up children were of the right age, Susan would work again, because she knew, and so did he, what happened to women of fifty at the height of their energy and ability, with grown-up children who no longer needed their full devotion.

So here was this couple, testing their marriage, looking after it, treating it like a small boat full of helpless people in a very stormy sea. Well, of course, so it was . . . The storms of the world were bad, but not too close – which is not to say they were selfishly felt, Susan and Matthew were both well-informed and responsible people. And the inner storms and quicksands were understood and charted. So everything was all right. Everything was in order. Yes, things were under control.

So what did it matter if they felt dry, flat. People like themselves, fed on a hundred books (psychological, anthropological, sociological) could scarcely be unprepared for the dry, controlled wistfulness which is the distinguishing mark of the intelligent marriage. Two people, endowed with education, with discrimination, with judgement, linked together voluntarily from their

will to be happy together and to be of use to others
. . . one sees them everywhere, one knows them, one
even is that thing oneself: sadness because so much is
after all so little. These two, unsurprised, turned
towards each other with even more courtesy and gentle
love: this was life, that two people, no matter how
carefully chosen, could not be everything to each other.
In fact, even to say so, to think in such a way, was
banal, they were ashamed to do it.

It was banal, too, when one night Matthew came
home late and confessed he had been to a party, taken
a girl home and slept with her. Susan forgave him,
of course. Except that forgiveness is hardly the word.
Understanding, yes. But if you understand something,
you don't forgive it, you are the thing itself: forgiveness
is for what you *don't* understand. Nor had he *confessed*
– what sort of word is that?

The whole thing was not important. After all, years
ago they had joked: of course I'm not going to be faithful to you, no one can be faithful to one other person
for a whole life-time. (And there was the word *faithful*
– stupid, all these words, stupid, belonging to a savage
old world.) But the incident left both of them irritable.
Strange, but they were both bad-tempered, annoyed.
There was something unassimilable about it.

Making love splendidly after he had come home that
night, both had felt that the idea that Myra Jenkins, a
pretty girl met at a party, could be even relevant, was
ridiculous. They had loved each other for over a
decade, would love each other for years more. Who,
then, was Myra Jenkins?

Except, thought Susan, unaccountably bad-
tempered, she was (is?) the first. In ten years. So either
the ten years' fidelity was not important, or she isn't.

(No, no, there is something wrong with this way of thinking, there must be.) But, if she isn't important, presumably it wasn't important either when Matthew and I first went to bed with each other that afternoon whose delight even now (like a very long shadow at sundown) lays a soft, wand-like finger over us. (Why did I say sundown?) Well, if what we felt that afternoon was not important, nothing is important, because if it hadn't been for what we felt, we wouldn't be Mr and Mrs Rawlings with four children, etc., etc. The whole thing is *absurd* – for him to have come home and told me was absurd. For him not to have told me was absurd. For me to care, or for that matter not to care is absurd . . . and who is Myra Jenkins? Why no one at all.

There was only one thing to do, and of course these sensible people did it: they put the thing behind them, and consciously, knowing what they were doing, moved forward into a different phase of their marriage, giving thanks for past good fortune as they did so.

For it was inevitable that the handsome, blond, attractive, manly man, Matthew Rawlings, should be at times tempted (oh, what a word!) by the attractive girls at parties she could not attend because of the four children; and that sometimes he would succumb (a word even more repulsive if possible) and that she, a good-looking woman in the big well-tended garden at Richmond would sometimes be pierced as by an arrow from the sky with bitterness. Except that bitterness was not in order, it was out of court. Did the casual girls touch the marriage? They did not. Rather it was they who knew defeat because of the handsome Matthew Rawlings's marriage body and soul to Susan Rawlings.

In that case why did Susan feel (though luckily not

for longer than a few seconds at a time) as if life had become a desert, and that nothing mattered, and that her children were not her own?

Meanwhile, her intelligence continued to assert that all was well. What if her Matthew did have an occasional sweet afternoon, the odd affair? For she knew quite well, except in her moments of aridity, that they were happy, that the affairs were not important.

Perhaps that was the trouble? It was in the nature of things that the adventures and delights could no longer be hers, because of the four children and the big house that needed so much attention. But perhaps she was secretly wishing, and even knowing that she did, that the wildness and the beauty could be his. But he was married to her. She was married to him. They were married inextricably. And therefore the gods could not strike him with the real magic, not really. Well, was it Susan's fault that after he came home from an adventure he looked harassed rather than fulfilled? (In fact, that was how she knew he had been *unfaithful*, because of his sullen air, and his glances at her, similar to hers at him: what is it that I share with this person that shields all delight from me?) But none of it was anybody's fault. (But what, did they feel, ought to be somebody's fault?) Nobody's fault, nothing to be at fault, no one to blame, no one to offer or to take it . . . and nothing wrong, either, except that Matthew never was really struck, as he wanted to be, by joy; and that Susan was more and more often threatened by emptiness. (It was usually in the garden that she was invaded by this feeling: she was coming to avoid the garden, unless the children or Matthew were with her.) There was no need to use the dramatic words, unfaithful, forgive, and the rest: intelligence forbade them. Intelligence barred,

112

too, quarrelling, sulking, anger, silences of withdrawal, accusations and tears. Above all, intelligence forbids tears.

A high price has to be paid for the happy marriage with the four healthy children in the large white gardened house.

And they were paying it, willingly, knowing what they were doing. When they lay side by side, or breast to breast in the big civilized bedroom overlooking the wild sullied river, they laughed, often, for no particular reason; but they knew it was really because of these two small people, Susan and Matthew, supporting such an edifice on their intelligent love. The laugh comforted them; it saved them both, though from what, they did not know.

They were now both forty-ish. The older children, boy and girl, were ten and eight, at school. The twins, six, were still at home. Susan did not have nurses or girls to help her: childhood is short; and she did not regret the hard work. Often enough she was bored, since small children can be boring; she was often very tired; but she regretted nothing. In another decade, she would turn herself back into being a woman with a life of her own.

Soon the twins would go to school, and they would be away from home from nine until four. These hours, so Susan saw it, would be the preparation for her own slow emancipation away from the rôle of hub-of-the-family into woman-with-her-own-life. She was already planning for the hours of freedom when all the children would be 'off her hands'. That was the phrase used by Matthew and by Susan and by their friends, for the moment when the youngest child went off to school. 'They'll be off your hands, darling Susan, and you'll have time to yourself.' So said Matthew, the intelligent husband, who had often enough commended and consoled Susan, standing by her in spirit during the years when her soul was not her own, as she said, but her children's.

What it amounted to was that Susan saw herself as she had been at twenty-eight, unmarried; and then again somewhere about fifty, blossoming from the root of what she had been twenty years before. As if the essential Susan was in abeyance, as if she were in cold storage. Matthew said something like this to Susan one night: and she agreed that it was true – she did feel something like that. What, then, was this essential Susan? She did not know. Put like that it sounded ridiculous, and she did not really feel it. Anyway, they had a long discussion about the whole thing before going off to sleep in each other's arms.

So the twins went off to their school, two bright affectionate children who had no problems about it, since their older brother and sister had trodden this path so successfully before them. And now Susan was going to be alone in the big house, every day of the school-term, except for the daily woman who came in to clean.

It was now, for the first time in this marriage, that something happened which neither of them had foreseen.

This is what happened. She returned, at nine-thirty, from taking the twins to the school by car, looking forward to seven blissful hours of freedom. On the first morning she was simply restless, worrying about the twins 'naturally enough' since this was their first day away at school. She was hardly able to contain herself until they came back. Which they did happily, excited by the world of school, looking forward to the next

114

day. And the next day Susan took them, dropped them, came back, and found herself reluctant to enter her big and beautiful home because it was as if something was waiting for her there that she did not wish to confront. Sensibly, however, she parked the car in the garage, entered the house, spoke to Mrs Parkes the daily woman about her duties, and went up to her bedroom. She was possessed by a fever which drove her out again, downstairs, into the kitchen, where Mrs Parkes was making cake and did not need her, and into the garden. There she sat on a bench and tried to calm herself, looking at trees, at a brown glimpse of the river. But she was filled with tension, like a panic: as if an enemy was in the garden with her. She spoke to herself severely, thus: All this is quite natural. First, I spent twelve years of my adult life working, *living my own life*. Then I married, and from the moment I became pregnant for the first time I signed myself over, so to speak, to other people. To the children. Not for one moment in twelve years have I been alone, had time to myself. So now I have to learn to be myself again. That's all.

And she went indoors to help Mrs Parkes cook and clean, and found some sewing to do for the children. She kept herself occupied every day. At the end of the first term she understood she felt two contrary emotions. First: secret astonishment and dismay that during those weeks when the house was empty of children she had, in fact, been more occupied (had been careful to keep herself occupied) than ever she had been when the children were around her needing her continual attention. Second: that now she knew the house would be full of them, and for five weeks, she resented the fact she would never be alone. She was already looking back at those hours of sewing, cooking (but by herself) as at a lost freedom which would not be hers for five long weeks. And the two months of term which would succeed the five weeks stretched alluringly open to her – freedom. But what freedom? – when, in fact, she had been so careful *not* to be free of small duties during the last weeks? She looked at herself, Susan Rawlings, sitting in a big chair by the window in the bedroom, sewing shirts or dresses, which she might just as well have bought. She saw herself making cakes for hours at a time in the big family kitchen: yet usually she bought cakes. What she saw was a woman alone, that was true, but she had not felt alone. For instance, Mrs Parkes was always somewhere in the house. And she did not like being in the garden at all, because of the closeness there of the enemy – irritation, restlessness, emptiness, whatever it was, that keeping her hands occupied made less dangerous for some reason.

Susan did not tell Matthew of these thoughts. They were not sensible. She did not recognize herself in them. What should she say to her dear friend and husband Matthew: 'When I go into the garden, that is, if the children are not there, I feel as if there is an enemy there waiting to invade me.' 'What enemy, Susan darling?' 'Well, I don't know, really . . .' 'Perhaps you should see a doctor?'

No, clearly this conversation should not take place. The holidays began and Susan welcomed them. Four children, lively, energetic, intelligent, demanding: she was never, not for a moment of her day, alone. If she were in a room, they would be in the next room, or waiting for her to do something for them; or it would soon be time for lunch or tea, or to take one of them to the dentist. Something to do: five weeks of it, thank goodness.

On the fourth day of these so welcome holidays, she found she was storming with anger at the twins, two shrinking beautiful children who (and this is what checked her) stood hand in hand looking at her with sheer dismayed disbelief. This was their calm mother, shouting at them. And for what? They had come to her with some game, some bit of nonsense. They looked at each other, moved closer for support, and went off hand in hand, leaving Susan holding on to the window-sill of the living-room, breathing deep, feeling sick. She went to lie down, telling the older children she had a headache. She heard the boy Harry telling the little ones: 'It's all right, mother's got a headache.' She heard that *it's all right* with pain.

That night she said to her husband: 'Today I shouted at the twins, quite unfairly.' She sounded miserable, and he said gently: 'Well, what of it?'

'It's more of an adjustment than I thought, their going to school.'

'But, Susie, Susie darling . . .' For she was crouched weeping on the bed. He comforted her: 'Susan, what is all this about? You shouted at them? What of it? If you shouted at them fifty times a day it wouldn't be more than the little devils deserve.' But she wouldn't laugh. She wept. Soon he comforted her with his body. She became calm. Calm, she wondered what was wrong with her, and why she should mind so much that she might, just once, have behaved unjustly with the children. What did it matter? They had forgotten it all long ago: mother had a headache and everything was all right.

It was a long time later that Susan understood that

117

that night, when she had wept and Matthew had driven the misery out of her with his big solid body, was the last time, in their married life, that they had been, to use their mutual language – with each other. And even that was a lie, because she had not told him of her real fears at all.

The five weeks passed, and Susan was in control of herself, and good and kind, and she looked forward to the end of the holidays with a mixture of fear and longing. She did not know what to expect. She took the twins off to school (the elder children took themselves to school) and she returned to the house determined to face the enemy wherever he was, in the house, or the garden or – where?

She was again restless, she was possessed by restlessness. She cooked and sewed and worked as before, day after day, while Mrs Parkes remonstrated: Mrs Rawlings, what's the need for it? I can do that, it's what you pay me for.

And it was so irrational, that she checked herself. She would put the car in the garage, go up to her bedroom, and sit, hands in her lap, forcing herself to be quiet. She listened to Mrs Parkes moving around the house. She looked out into the garden and saw the branches shake the trees. She sat defeating the enemy, restlessness. Emptiness. She ought to be thinking about her life, about herself. But she did not. Or perhaps she could not. As soon as she forced her mind to think about Susan (for what else did she want to be alone for?) it skipped off to thoughts of butter or school clothes. Or it thought of Mrs Parkes. She realized that she sat listening for the movements of the cleaning woman, following her every turn, bend, thought. She followed her in mind from kitchen to bathroom, from table to oven, and it was as if the duster, the cleaning cloth, the saucepan, were in her own hand. She would hear herself saying: No, not like that, don't put that there . . . Yet she did not give a damn what Mrs Parkes did, or if she did it at all. Yet she could not prevent herself from being conscious of her every minute. Yes, this was what was wrong with her: she needed, when she was alone, to be really alone, with no one near. She could not endure the knowledge that in ten minutes or in half an hour Mrs Parkes would call up the stairs: Mrs Rawlings, there's no silver polish, Madam, we're out of flour.

So she left the house and went to sit in the garden where she was screened from the house by trees. She waited for the demon to appear and claim her, but he did not.

She was keeping him off, because she had not, after all, come to an end of arranging herself.

She was planning how to be somewhere where Mrs Parkes would not come after her with a cup of tea, or a demand to be allowed to telephone (always irritating since Susan did not care who she telephoned or how often) or just a nice talk about something. Yes, she needed a place, or a state of affairs where it would not be necessary to keep reminding herself: In ten minutes I must telephone Matthew about . . . and at half past three I must leave early for the children because the car needs cleaning. And at ten o'clock tomorrow I must remember – She was possessed with resentment that the seven hours of freedom in every day (during week-days in the school-term) were not free, that never, not for one second, ever, was she free from the pressure of time, from having to remember this or that. She could never forget herself; never really let herself go into forgetfulness.

Resentment. It was poisoning her. (She looked at this emotion and thought it was absurd.) Yet she felt it. She was a prisoner . . . (She looked at this thought, too, and it was no good telling herself it was a ridiculous one.) She must tell Matthew – but what? She was filled with emotions that were utterly ridiculous, that she despised, yet that nevertheless she was feeling so strongly she could not shake them off.

The school holidays came round, and this time they were for nearly two months, and she behaved with a conscious controlled decency that nearly drove her crazy. She would lock herself in the bathroom, and sit on the edge of the bath, breathing deep, trying to let go into some kind of calm. Or she went up into the spare room, usually empty, where no one would expect her to be. She heard the children calling Mother, Mother, and kept silent, feeling guilty. Or she went to the very end of the garden, by herself, and looked at the slow-moving brown river; she looked at the river and closed her eyes and breathed slow and deep, taking it into her being, into her veins.

Then she returned to the family, wife and mother, smiling and responsible, feeling as if the pressure of these people – four lively children and her husband, were a painful pressure on the surface of her skin, a hand pressing on her brain. She did not break down into irritation during these holidays, but it was like living out a prison sentence, and when the children went back to school, she sat on a white stone seat near the flowing river, and she thought: It is not even a year since the twins went to school, since *they were off my hands* (what on earth did I think I meant when I used that stupid phrase?) and yet I'm a different person. I'm simply not myself. I don't understand it.

Yet she had to understand it. For she knew that this structure – big white house, on which the mortgage still cost four hundred a year, a husband, so good and kind and insightful, four children, all doing so nicely, and the garden where she sat, and Mrs Parkes the cleaning woman – all this depended on her, and yet she could not understand why, or even what it was she contributed to it.

She said to Matthew in their bedroom: 'I think there must be something wrong with me.'

And he said: 'Surely not, Susan? You look marvellous – you're as lovely as ever.'

She looked at the handsome blond man, with his clear, intelligent, blue-eyed face, and thought: Why is it I can't tell him? Why not? And she said: 'I need to be alone more than I am.'

At which he swung his slow blue gaze at her, and she saw what she had been dreading: Incredulity. Disbelief. And fear. An incredulous blue stare from a stranger who was her husband, as close to her as her own breath.

He said: 'But the children are at school and off your hands.'

She said to herself: I've got to force myself to say: Yes, but do you realize that I never feel free? There's never a moment I can say to myself: 'There's nothing I have to remind myself about, nothing I have to do in half an hour, or an hour, or two hours . . .'

But she said: 'I don't feel well.'

He said: 'Perhaps you need a holiday.'

She said, appalled: 'But not without you, surely?' For she could not imagine herself going off without him. Yet that was what he meant. Seeing her face, he laughed, and opened his arms, and she went into them, thinking: Yes, yes, but why can't I say it? And what is it I have to say?

She tried to tell him, about never being free. And he listened and said: 'But, Susan, what sort of freedom can you possible want – short of being dead! Am I ever free? I go to the office, and I have to be there at ten – all right, half past ten, sometimes. And I have to do this or that, don't I? Then I've got to come home at a certain time – I don't mean it, you know I don't – but if I'm not going to be back home at six I'll telephone you. When can I ever say to myself: I have nothing to be responsible for in the next six hours?'

Susan, hearing this, was remorseful. Because it was true. The good marriage, the house, the children, depended just as much on his voluntary bondage as it did on hers. But why did he not feel bound? Why didn't he chafe and become restless? No, there was something really wrong with her and this proved it.

And that word *bondage* – why had she used it? She had never felt marriage, or the children, as bondage. Neither had he, or surely they wouldn't be together lying in each other's arms content after twelve years of marriage.

No, her state (whatever it was) was irrelevant, nothing to do with her real good life with her family. She had to accept the fact that, after all, she was an irrational person and to live with it. Some people had to live with crippled arms, or stammers, or being deaf. She would have to live knowing she was subject to a state of mind she could not own.

Nevertheless, as a result of this conversation with her husband, there was a new régime next holidays.

The spare room at the top of the house now had a

cardboard sign saying: Private! Do not Disturb! on it. (This sign had been drawn in coloured chalks by the children, after a discussion between the parents in which it was decided this was psychologically the right thing.) The family and Mrs Parkes knew this was 'Mother's Room' and that she was entitled to her privacy. Many serious conversations took place between Matthew and the children about not taking mother for granted. Susan overheard the first, between father and Harry, the older boy, and was surprised at her irritation over it. Surely she could have a room somewhere in that big house and retire into it without such a fuss being made? Without it being so solemnly discussed? Why couldn't she simply have announced: 'I'm going to fit out the little top room for myself, and when I'm in it I'm not to be disturbed for anything short of fire?' Just that, and finished; instead of long, earnest discussions. When she heard Harry and Matthew explaining it to the twins with Mrs Parkes coming in: 'Yes, well a family sometimes gets on top of a woman . . .' she had to go right away to the bottom of the garden until the devils of exasperation had finished their dance in her blood.

But now there was a room, and she could go there when she liked, she used it seldom: she felt even more caged there than in her bedroom. One day she had gone up there after a lunch for ten children she had cooked and served because Mrs Parkes was not there, and had sat alone for a while looking into the garden. She saw the children stream out from the kitchen and stand looking up at the window where she sat behind the curtains. They were all – her children and their friends – discussing Mother's Room. A few minutes later, the chase of children in some game came pounding up the stairs, but ended as abruptly as if they had fallen over a ravine, so sudden was the silence. They had remembered she was there, and had gone silent in a great hale of Hush! Shhhhh, Quiet, you'll disturb her . . . And they went tip-toeing downstairs like criminal conspirators. When she came down to make tea for them, they all apologized. The twins put their arms around her, from front to back, making a human cage of loving limbs, and promised it would never occur again. 'We forgot, Mummy, we forgot all about it!'

What it amounted to was that Mother's Room, and her need for privacy had become a valuable lesson in respect for other people's rights. Quite soon Susan was going up to the room only because it was a lesson it was a pity to drop. Then she took sewing up there, and the children and Mrs Parkes came in and out: it had become another family room.

She sighed, and smiled, and resigned herself – she made jokes at her own expense with Matthew over the room. That is, she did from the self she liked, she respected. But at the same time, something inside her howled with impatience, with rage . . . And she was frightened. One day she found herself kneeling by her bed and praying: 'Dear God, keep it away from me, keep him away from me.' She meant, the devil, for she now thought of it, not caring if she were irrational, as some sort of demon. She imagined him, or it, as a youngish man, or perhaps a middle-aged man pretending to be young. Or a man young-looking from immaturity? At any rate, she saw the young-looking face which, when she drew closer, had dry lines about mouth and eyes. He was thinnish, meagre in build. And he had a reddish complexion, and ginger hair. That was he – a gingery, energetic man, and he wore a reddish hairy jacket, unpleasant to the touch.

Well, one day she saw him. She was standing at the bottom of the garden, watching the river ebb past, when she raised her eyes and saw this person, or being, sitting on the white stone bench. He was looking at her, and grinning. In his hand was a long crooked stick, which he had picked off the ground, or broken off the tree above him. He was absent-mindedly, out of an absent-minded or freakish impulse of spite, using the stick to stir around in the coils of a blindworm or a grass-snake (or some kind of snake-like creature: it was whitish and unhealthy to look at, unpleasant). The snake was twisting about, flinging its coils from side to side in a kind of dance of protest against the teasing prodding stick.

Susan looked at him thinking: Who is the stranger? What is he doing in our garden? Then she recognized the man around whom her terrors had crystallized. As she did so, he vanished. She made herself walk over to the bench. A shadow from a branch lay across thin emerald grass, moving jerkily over its roughness, and she could see why she had taken it for a snake, lashing and twisting. She went back to the house thinking: Right then, so I've seen him with my own eyes, so I'm not crazy after all – there *is* a danger because I've seen him. He is lurking in the garden and sometimes even in the house, and he wants *to get into me and to take me over*.

She dreamed of having a room or a place, anywhere, where she could go and sit, by herself, no one knowing where she was.

Once, near Victoria, she found herself outside a newsagent that had Rooms to Let advertised. She decided to rent a room, telling no one. Sometimes she could take the train in from Richmond and sit alone in it for an hour or two. Yet how could she? A room would cost three or four pounds a week, and she earned no money, and how could she explain to Matthew that she needed such a sum. What for? It did not occur to her that she was taking it for granted she wasn't going to tell him about the room.

Well, it was out of the question, having a room; yet she knew she must.

One day, when a school-term was well-established, and none of the children had measles or other ailments, and everything seemed in order, she did the shopping early, explained to Mrs Parkes she was meeting an old school-friend, took the train to Victoria, searched until she found a small quiet hotel, and asked for a room for the day. They did not let rooms by the day, the manageress said, looking doubtful, since Susan so obviously was not the kind of woman who needed a room for unrespectable reasons. Susan made a long explanation about not being well, being unable to shop without frequent rests for lying down. At last she was allowed to rent the room provided she paid a full night's price for it. She was taken up by the manageress and a maid, both concerned over the state of her health . . . which must be pretty bad if, living at Richmond (she had signed her name and address in the register) she needed a shelter at Victoria.

The room was ordinary and anonymous, and was just what Susan needed. She put a shilling in the gas fire, and sat, eyes shut, in a dingy armchair with her back to a dingy window. She was alone. She was alone. She was alone. She could feel pressures lifting off her. First the sounds of traffic came very loud; then they seemed to vanish; she might even have slept a little. A knock on the door: it was Miss Townsend the manageress, bringing her a cup of tea with her own hands, so concerned was she over Susan's long silence and possible illness.

Miss Townsend was a lonely woman of fifty, running this hotel with all the rectitude expected of her, and she sensed in Susan the possibility of understanding companionship. She stayed to talk. Susan found herself in the middle of a fantastic story about her illness, which got more and more improbable as she tried to make it tally with the large house at Richmond, well-off husband, and four children. Suppose she said instead: Miss Townsend, I'm here in your hotel because I need to be alone for a few hours, above all *alone and with no one knowing where I am*. She said it mentally, and saw, mentally, the look that would inevitably come on Miss Townsend's elderly maiden's face. 'Miss Townsend, my four children and my husband are driving me insane, do you understand that? Yes, I can see from the gleam of hysteria in your eyes that comes from loneliness controlled but only just contained that I've got everything in the world you've ever longed for. Well, Miss Townsend, I don't want any of it. You can have it, Miss Townsend. I wish I was absolutely alone in the world, like you. Miss Townsend, I'm besieged by seven devils, Miss Townsend, Miss Townsend, let me stay here in your hotel where the devils can't get me . . .' Instead of saying all this, she described her anaemia, agreed to try Miss Townsend's remedy for it, which was raw liver, minced, between wholemeal bread, and said yes, perhaps it would be better if she stayed at home and let a friend do shopping for her. She paid her bill and left the hotel, defeated.

At home Mrs Parkes said she didn't really like it, no, not really, when Mrs Rawlings was away from nine in the morning until five. The teacher had telephoned from school to say Joan's teeth were paining her, and she hadn't known what to say; and what was she to make for the children's tea, Mrs Rawlings hadn't said.

All this was nonsense, of course. Mrs Parkes's complaint was that Susan had withdrawn herself spiritually, leaving the burden of the big house on her.

Susan looked back at her day of 'freedom' which had resulted in her becoming a friend to the lonely Miss Townsend, and in Mrs Parkes's remonstrances. Yet she remembered the short blissful hour of being alone, really alone. She was determined to arrange her life, no matter what it cost, so that she could have that solitude more often. An absolute solitude, where no one knew her or cared about her.

But how? She thought of saying to her old employer: I want you to back me up in a story with Matthew that I am doing part-time work for you. The truth is that . . . but she would have to tell him a lie too, and which lie? She could not say: I want to sit by myself three or four times a week in a rented room. And besides, he knew Matthew, and she could not really ask him to tell lies on her behalf, apart from his being bound to think it meant a lover.

Suppose she really took a part-time job, which she could get through fast and efficiently, leaving time for herself. What job? Addressing envelopes? Canvassing?

And there was Mrs Parkes, working widow, who knew exactly what she was prepared to give to the house, who knew by instinct when her mistress withdrew in spirit from her responsibilities. Mrs Parkes was one of the servers of this world, but she needed someone to serve. She had to have Mrs Rawlings, her madam, at the top of the house or in the garden, so that she could come and get support from her: 'Yes, the bread's not what it was when I was a girl, yes, Harry's got a wonderful appetite, I wonder where he puts it all, yes it's lucky the twins are so much of a size, they can wear each other's shoes, that's a saving in these hard times, yes, the cherry jam from Switzerland is not a patch on the jam from Poland, and three times the price . . .' And so on. That sort of talk Mrs Parkes must have, every day, or she would leave, not knowing herself why she left.

Susan Rawlings, thinking these thoughts, found that she was prowling through the great thicketed garden like a wild cat: she was walking up the stairs, down the stairs, through the rooms, into the garden, along the brown running river, back, up through the house, down again . . . it was a wonder Mrs Parkes did not think it strange. But, on the contrary, Mrs Rawlings could do what she liked, she could stand on her head if she wanted, provided she was *there*. Susan Rawlings prowled and muttered through her house, hating Mrs Parkes, hating poor Miss Townsend, dreaming of her hour of solitude in the dingy respectability of Miss Townsend's hotel bedroom, and she knew quite well she was mad. Yes, she was mad!

She said to Matthew that she must have a holiday. Matthew agreed with her. This was not as things had been once – how they talked in each other's arms in the marriage bed. He had, she knew, diagnosed her finally as *unreasonable*. She had become someone outside himself that he had to manage. They were living side by side in this house like two tolerably friendly strangers.

Having told Mrs Parkes, or rather, asked for her permission, she went off on a walking holiday in Wales. She chose the remotest place she knew of. Every morning the children telephoned her before they went off to school, to encourage and support her, just as they had over Mother's Room. Every evening she telephoned them, spoke to each child in turn, and then to Matthew. Mrs Parkes, given permission to telephone for instructions or advice, did so every day at lunchtime. When, as happened three times, Mrs Rawlings was out on the mountainside, Mrs Parkes asked that she should ring back at such-and-such a time, for she would not be happy in what she was doing without Mrs Rawlings's blessing.

Susan prowled over wild country with the telephone wire holding her to her duty like a leash. The next time she must telephone, or wait to be telephoned, nailed her to her cross. The mountains themselves seemed trammelled by her unfreedom. Everywhere on the mountains, where she met no one at all, from breakfast-time to dusk, excepting sheep, or a shepherd, she came face to face with her own craziness which might attack her in the broadest valleys, so that they seemed too small; or on a mountain-top from which she could see a hundred other mountains and valleys, so that they seemed too low, too small, with the sky pressing down too close. She would stand gazing at a hill-side brilliant with ferns and bracken, jewelled with running water, and see nothing but her devil, who lifted inhuman eyes at her from where he leaned negligently on a rock, switching at his ugly yellow boots with a leafy twig.

She returned to her home and family, with the Welsh emptiness at the back of her mind like a promise of freedom.

She told her husband she wanted to have an *au pair* girl.

They were in their bedroom, it was late at night, the children slept. He sat, shirted and slippered, in a chair by the window, looking out. She sat brushing her hair and watching him in the mirror. A time-hallowed scene in the connubial bedroom. He said nothing, while she heard the arguments coming into his mind, only to be rejected because every one was *reasonable*. 'It seems strange to get one now, after all, the children are at school most of the day. Surely the time for you to have help was when you were stuck with them day and night. Why don't you ask Mrs Parkes to cook for you, she's even offered to – I can understand if you are tired of cooking for six people. But you know that an *au pair* girls means all kinds of problems, it's not like having an ordinary char in during the day . . .'

Finally he said carefully: 'Are you thinking of going back to work?'

'No,' she said, 'no, not really.' She made herself sound vague, rather stupid. She went on brushing her black hair and peering at herself so as to be oblivious of the short, uneasy glances her Matthew kept giving her. 'Do you think we can't afford it,' she went on vaguely, not at all the old efficient Susan who knew exactly what they could afford.

'It's not that,' he said, looking out of the window at dark trees, so as not to look at her. Meanwhile, she examined a round, candid, pleasant face with clear dark brows and clear grey eyes. A sensible face. She brushed thick healthy black hair and thought: Yet that's the reflection of a mad woman. How very strange! Much more to the point if what looked back at me was the gingery green-eyed demon with his dry meagre smile

. . . why wasn't Matthew agreeing? After all, what else could he do? She was breaking her part of the bargain and there was no way of forcing her to keep it: that her spirit, her soul, should live in this house, so that the people in it could grow like plants in water, and Mrs Parkes remain content in their service. In return for this, he would be a good loving husband, and responsible towards the children. Well, nothing like this had been true of either of them for a long time. He did his duty, perfunctorily; she did not even pretend to do hers. And he had become like other husbands, with his real life in his work and the people he met there, and very likely a serious affair. All this was her fault.

At last he drew heavy curtains, blotting out the trees, and turned to force her attention: 'Susan, are you really sure we need a girl?' But she would not meet his appeal at all: she was running the brush over her hair again and again, lifting fine black clouds in a small hiss of electricity. She was peering in and smiling as if she were amused at the clinging hissing hair that followed the brush.

'Yes, I think it would be a good idea on the whole,' she said, with the cunning of a madwoman evading the real point.

In the mirror she could see her Matthew lying on his back, his hands behind his head, staring upwards, his face sad and hard. She felt her heart (the old heart of Susan Rawlings) soften and call out to him. But she set it to be indifferent.

He said: 'Susan, the children?' It was an appeal that *almost* reached her. He opened his arms, lifting them from where they had lain by his sides, palms up, empty. She had only to run across and fling herself into them, on to his hard, warm chest, and melt into herself, into

Susan. But she could not. She would not see his lifted arms. She said vaguely: 'Well, surely it'll be even better for them? We'll get a French or a German girl and they'll learn the language.'

In the dark she lay beside him, feeling frozen, a stranger. She felt as if Susan had been spirited away. She disliked very much this woman who lay here, cold and indifferent beside a suffering man, but she could not change her.

Next morning she set about getting a girl, and very soon came Sophie Traub from Hamburg, a girl of twenty, laughing, healthy, blue-eyed, intending to learn English. Indeed, she already spoke a good deal. In return for a room, 'Mother's Room', and her food, she undertook to do some light cooking, and to be with the children when Mrs Rawlings asked. She was an intelligent girl and understood perfectly what was needed. Susan said: 'I go off sometimes, for the morning or for the day – well, sometimes the children run home from school, or they ring up, or a teacher rings up. I should be here, really. And there's the daily woman . . .' And Sophie laughed her deep fruity fräulein's laugh, showed her fine white teeth and her dimples, and said: 'You want some person to play mistress of the house sometimes, not so?'

'Yes, that is just so,' said Susan, a bit dry, despite herself, thinking in secret fear how easy it was, how much nearer to the end she was than she thought. Healthy Fräulein Traub's instant understanding of their position proved this to be true.

The *au pair* girl, because of her own common sense, or (as Susan said to herself with her new inward shudder) because she had been *chosen* so well by Susan, was a success with everyone, the children liking her,

Mrs Parkes forgetting almost at once that she was German, and Matthew finding her 'nice to have around the house'. For he was now taking things as they came, from the surface of life, withdrawn both as a husband and a father from the household.

One day Susan saw how Sophie and Mrs Parkes were talking and laughing in the kitchen, and she announced that she would be away until tea-time. She knew exactly where to go and what she must look for. She took the District Line to South Kensington, changed to the Circle, got off at Paddington, and walked around looking at the smaller hotels until she was satisfied with one which had 'Fred's Hotel' painted on window-panes that needed cleaning. The façade was a faded shiny yellow, like unhealthy skin. A door at the end of a passage said she must knock; she did, and Fred appeared. He was not at all attractive, not in any way, being fattish, and run-down, and wearing a tasteless striped suit. He had small sharp eyes in a white creased face, and was quite prepared to let Mrs Jones (she chose the farcical name deliberately, staring him out) have a room three days a week from ten until six. Provided, of course, that she paid in advance each time she came? Susan produced fifteen shillings (no price had been set by him) and held it out, still fixing him with a bold unblinking challenge she had not known until then she could use at will. Looking at her still, he took up a ten shilling note from her palm between thumb and forefinger, fingered it; then shuffled up two half-crowns, held out his own palm with these bits of money displayed thereon, and let his gaze lower broodingly at them. They were standing in the passage, a red-shaded light above, bare boards beneath, and a strong smell of floor polish rising about them. He shot his gaze up at her over the still-extended palm, and smiled as if to say: What do you take me for? 'I shan't,' said Susan, 'be using this room for the purposes of making money.' He still waited. She added another five shillings, at which he nodded and said: 'You pay, and I ask no questions.' 'Good,' said Susan. He now went past her to the stairs, and there waited a moment: the light from the street door being in her eyes, she lost sight of him momentarily. Then she saw a sober-suited, white-faced, white-balding little man trotting up the stairs like a waiter, and she went after him. They proceeded in utter silence up the stairs of this house where no questions were asked – 'Fred's Hotel,' which could afford the freedom for its visitors that poor Miss Townsend's hotel could not. The room was hideous. It had a single window, with thin green brocade curtains, a three-quarter bed that had a cheap green satin bedspread on it, a fireplace with a gas-fire and a shilling meter by it, a chest of drawers, and a green wicker armchair.

'Thank you,' said Susan, knowing that Fred (if this was Fred, and not George, or Herbert or Charlie) was looking at her, not so much with curiosity, an emotion he would not own to, for professional reasons, but with a philosophical sense of what was appropriate. Having taken her money and shown her up and agreed to everything, he was clearly disapproving of her for coming here. She did not belong here at all, so his look said. (But she knew, already, how very much she did belong: the room had been waiting for her to join it.) 'Would you have me called at five o'clock, please?' and he nodded and went downstairs.

It was twelve in the morning. She was free. She sat in the armchair, she simply sat, she closed her eyes and sat and let herself be alone. She was alone and no one knew where she was. When a knock came on the door she was annoyed, and prepared to show it: but it was Fred himself, it was five o'clock and he was calling her as ordered. He flicked his sharp little eyes over the room – bed, first. It was undisturbed. She might never have been in the room at all. She thanked him, said she would be returning the day after tomorrow, and left. She was back home in time to cook supper, to put the children to bed, to cook a second supper for her husband and herself later. And to welcome Sophie back from the pictures where she had gone with a friend. All these things she did cheerfully, willingly. But she was thinking all the time of the hotel room, she was longing for it with her whole being.

Three times a week. She arrived promptly at ten, looked Fred in the eyes, gave him twenty shillings, followed him up the stairs, went into the room, and shut the door on him with gentle firmness. For Fred, disapproving of her being here at all, was quite ready to let friendship, or at least acquaintanceship, follow his disapproval, if only she would let him. But he was content to go off on her dismissing nod with the twenty shillings in his hand.

She sat in the armchair and shut her eyes.

What did she *do* in the room? Why, nothing at all. From the chair, when it had rested her, she went to the window, stretching her arms, smiling, treasuring her anonymity, to look out. She was no longer Susan Rawlings, mother of four, wife of Matthew, employer of Mrs Parkes and of Sophie Traub, with these and those relations with friends, school-teachers, tradesmen. She no longer was mistress of the big white house and garden, owning clothes suitable for this and that activity or occasion. She was Mrs Jones, and she was alone,

136

and she had no past and no future. Here I am, she thought, after all these years of being married and having children and playing those rôles of responsibility – and I'm just the same. Yet there have been times I thought that nothing existed of me except the rôles that went with being Mrs Matthew Rawlings. Yes, here I am, and if I never saw any of my family again, here I would still be . . . how very strange this is! And she leaned on the sill, and looked into the street, loving the men and women who passed, because she did not know them. She looked at the downtrodden buildings over the street, and at the sky, wet and dingy, or sometimes blue, and she felt she had never seen buildings or sky before. And then she went back to the chair, empty, her mind a blank. Sometimes she talked aloud, saying nothing – an exclamation, meaningless, followed by a comment about the floral pattern on the thin rug, or a stain on the green satin coverlet. For the most part, she wool-gathered – what word is there for it? – brooded, wandered, simply went dark, feeling emptiness run deliciously through her veins like the movement of her blood.

This room had become more her own than the house she lived in. One morning she found Fred taking her a flight higher than usual. She stopped, refusing to go up, and demanded her usual room, number 19. 'Well, you'll have to wait half an hour, then,' he said. Willingly she descended to the dark disinfectant-smelling hall, and sat waiting until the two, man and woman, came down the stairs, giving her swift indifferent glances before they hurried out into the street, separating at the door. She went up to the room, *her* room, which they had just vacated. It was no less hers, though the

137

windows were set wide open, and a maid was straightening the bed as she came in.

After these days of solitude, it was both easy to play her part as mother and wife, and difficult – because it was so easy: she felt an imposter. She felt as if her shell moved here, with her family, answering to Mummy, Mother, Susan, Mrs Rawlings. She was surprised no one saw through her, that she wasn't turned out of doors, as a fake. On the contrary, it seemed the children loved her more; Matthew and she 'got on' pleasantly, and Mrs Parkes was happy in her work under (for the most part, it must be confessed) Sophie Traub. At night she lay beside her husband, and they made love again, apparently just as they used to, when they were really married. But she, Susan, or the being who answered so readily and improbably to the name of Susan, was not there: she was in Fred's Hotel, in Paddington, waiting for the easing hours of solitude to begin.

Soon she made a new arrangement with Fred and with Sophie. It was for five days a week. As for the money, five pounds, she simply asked Matthew for it. She saw that she was not even frightened he might ask what for: he would give it to her, she knew that, and yet it was terrifying it could be so, for this close couple, these partners, had once known the destination of every shilling they must spend. He agreed to give her five pounds a week. She asked for just so much, not a penny more. He sounded indifferent about it. It was as if he were paying her, she thought: *paying her off* – yes, that was it. Terror came back for a moment, when she understood this, but she stilled it: things had gone too far for that. Now, every week, on Sunday nights, he gave her five pounds, turning away from her before their eyes could meet on the transaction. As for Sophie Traub, she was to be somewhere in or near the house until six at night, after which she was free. She was not to cook or to clean, she was simply to be there. So she gardened or sewed, and asked friends in, being a human being who was bound to have a lot of friends. If the children were sick, she nursed them. If teachers telephoned, she answered them sensibly. For the five daytimes in the school week, she was altogether the mistress of the house.

One night in the bedroom, Matthew asked: 'Susan, I don't want to interfere, don't think that, please, but are you sure you are well?'

She was brushing her hair at the mirror. She made two more strokes on either side of her head, before she replied: 'Yes, dear, I am sure I am well.'

He was again lying on his back, his big blond head on his hands, his elbows angled up and part-concealing his face. He said: 'Then, Susan, I have to ask you this question, though you must understand, I'm not putting any sort of pressure on you . . .' (Susan heard the word pressure with dismay, because this was inevitable, of course she could not go on like this) '. . . are things going to go on like this?'

'Well,' she said, going vague and bright and idiotic again, so as to escape, 'Well, I don't see why not.'

He was jerking his elbows up and down, in annoyance or in pain, and, looking at him, she saw he had got thin, even gaunt; and restless angry movements were not what she remembered of him. He said: 'Do you want a divorce, is that it?'

At this, Susan only with the greatest difficulty stopped herself from laughing: she could hear the bright bubbling laughter she *would* have emitted, had she let herself. He could only mean one thing: she had a lover, and that was why she spent her days in London, as lost to him as if she had vanished to another continent.

Then the small panic set in again: she understood that he hoped she did have a lover, he was begging her to say so, because otherwise it would be too terrifying.

She thought this out, as she brushed her hair, watching the fine black stuff fly up to make its little clouds of electricity, hiss, hiss, hiss: behind her head, across the room, was a blue wall. She realized she was absorbed in watching the black hair making shapes against the blue. She should be answering him. 'Do *you* want a divorce, Matthew?'

He said: 'That surely isn't the point, is it?'

'You brought it up, I didn't,' she said, brightly, suppressing meaningless tinkling laughter.

Next day she asked Fred: 'Have inquiries been made for me?'

He hesitated, and she said: 'I've been coming here a year now. I've made no trouble, and you've been paid every day. I have a right to be told.'

'As a matter of fact, Mrs Jones, a man did come asking.'

'A man from a detective agency?'

'Well, he could have been, couldn't he?'

'I was asking you . . . well, what did you tell him?'

'I told him a Mrs Jones came every weekday from ten until five or six and stayed in No. 19 by herself.'

'Describing me?'

'Well, Mrs Jones, I had no alternative, put yourself in my place?'

'By rights I should deduct what that man gave you for the information.'

He raised shocked eyes: she was not the sort of

140

person to make jokes like this! Then he chose to laugh: a pinkish wet slit appeared across his white crinkled face: his eyes positively begged her to laugh, otherwise he might lose some money. She remained grave, looking at him.

He stopped laughing and said: 'You want to go up now?' – returning to the familiarity, the comradeship, of the country where no questions are asked, on which (and he knew it) she depended completely.

She went up to sit in her wicker-chair. But it was not the same. Her husband had searched her out. (The world had searched her out.) The pressures were on her. She was here with his connivance. He might walk in at any moment, here, into Room 19. She imagined the report from the detective agency: 'A woman calling herself Mrs Jones, fitting the description of your wife (etc., etc., etc.) stays alone all day in Room No. 19. She insists on this room, waits for it if it is engaged. As far as the proprietor knows, she receives no visitors there, male or female.' A report something on these lines, Matthew must have received.

Well, of course he was right: things couldn't go on like this. He had put an end to it all simply by sending the detective after her.

She tried to shrink herself back into the shelter of the room, a snail pecked out of its shell and trying to squirm back. But the peace of the room had gone. She was trying consciously to revive it, trying to let go into the dark creative trance (or whatever it was) that she had found there. It was no use, yet she craved for it, she was as ill as a suddenly deprived addict.

Several times she returned to the room, to look for herself there, but instead she found the unnamed spirit of restlessness, a prickling fevered hunger for

141

movement, an irritable self-consciousness that made her brain feel as if it had coloured lights going on and off inside it. Instead of the soft dark that had been the room's air, were now waiting for her demons that made her dash blindly about, muttering words of hate; she was impelling herself from point to point like a moth dashing itself against a window-pane, sliding to the bottom, fluttering off on broken wings, then crashing into the invisible barrier again. And again and again. Soon she was exhausted, and she told Fred that for a while she would not be needing the room, she was going on holiday. Home she went, to the big white house by the river. The middle of a weekday, and she felt guilty at returning to her own home when not expected. She stood unseen, looking in at the kitchen window. Mrs Parkes, wearing a discarded floral overall of Susan's, was stooping to slide something into the oven. Sophie, arms folded, was leaning her back against a cupboard and laughing at some joke made by a girl not seen before by Susan – a dark foreign girl, Sophie's visitor. In an armchair Molly, one of the twins, lay curled sucking her thumb and watching the grown-ups. She must have some sickness, to be kept from school. The child's listless face, the dark circles under her eyes, hurt Susan: Molly was looking at the three grown-ups working and talking in exactly the same way Susan looked at the four through the kitchen window: she was remote, shut off from them.

But then, just as Susan imagined herself going in, picking up the little girl, and sitting in an armchair with her, stroking her probably heated forehead, Sophie did just that: she had been standing on one leg, the other knee flexed, its foot set against the wall. Now she let her foot in its ribbon-tied shoe slide down the wall, stood solid on two feet, clapping her hands before and behind her, and sang a couple of lines in German, so that the child lifted her heavy eyes at her and began to smile. Then she walked, or rather skipped over to the child, swung her up, and let her fall into her lap at the same moment she sat herself. She said 'Hopla! Hopla! Molly . . .' and began stroking the dark untidy young head that Molly laid on her shoulder for comfort.

Well . . . Susan blinked the tears of farewell out of her eyes, and went quietly up the house to her bedroom. There she sat looking at the river through the trees. She felt at peace, but in a way that was new to her. She had no desire to move, to talk, to do anything at all. The devils that had haunted the house, the garden, were not there; but she knew it was because her soul was in Room 19 in 'Fred's Hotel'; she was not really here at all. It was a sensation that should have been frightening: to sit at her own bedroom window, listening to Sophie's rich young voice sing German nursery songs to her child, listening to Mrs Parkes clatter and move below, and to know that all this had nothing to do with her: she was already out of it.

Later, she made herself go down and say she was home: it was unfair to be here unannounced. She took lunch with Mrs Parkes, Sophie, Sophie's Italian friend Maria, and her daughter Molly, and felt like a visitor.

A few days later, at bedtime, Matthew said: 'Here's your five pounds,' and pushed them over at her. Yet he must have known she had not been leaving the house at all.

She shook her head, gave it back to him, and said, in explanation, not in accusation: 'As soon as you knew where I was, there was no point.'

He nodded, not looking at her. He was turned away

from her: thinking, she knew, how best to handle this wife who terrified him.

He said: 'I wasn't trying to . . . it's just that I was worried.'

'Yes, I know.'

'I must confess that I was beginning to wonder . . .'

'You thought I had a lover?'

'Yes, I am afraid I did.'

She knew that he wished she had. She sat wondering how to say: 'For a year now I've been spending all my days in a very sordid hotel room. It's the place where I'm happy. In fact without it I don't exist.' She heard herself saying this, and understood how terrified he was that she might. So instead she said: 'Well, perhaps you're not far wrong.'

Probably Matthew would think the hotel proprietor lied: he would want to think so.

'Well,' he said, and she could hear his voice spring up, so to speak, with relief: 'in that case I must confess I've got a bit of an affair on myself.'

She said, detached and interested: 'Really? Who is she?' and saw Matthew's startled look because of this reaction.

'It's Phil. Phil Hunt.'

She had known Phil Hunt well in the old unmarried days. She was thinking: No, she won't do, she's too neurotic and difficult. She's never been happy yet. Sophie's much better: Well, Matthew will see that himself, sensible as he is.

This line of thought went on in silence, while she said aloud: 'It's no point telling you about mine, because you don't know him.'

Quick, quick, invent, she thought. Remember how you invented all that nonsense for Miss Townsend.

She began slowly, careful not to contradict herself: 'His name is Michael . . .' (*Michael what?*) '. . . Michael Plant.' (What a silly name!) 'He's rather like you – in looks, I mean.' And, indeed, she could imagine herself being touched by no one but Matthew himself. 'He's a publisher.' (Really? Why?) 'He's got a wife already and two children.'

She brought out this fantasy, proud of herself.

Matthew said: 'Are you thinking of marrying?'

She said, before she could stop herself: 'Good God, *no*!'

She realized, if Matthew wanted to marry Phil Hunt, that this was too emphatic, but apparently it was all right for his voice sounded relieved as he said: 'It is a bit impossible to imagine oneself married to anyone else, isn't it?' With which he pulled her to him so that her head lay on his shoulder. She turned her face into the dark of his flesh, and listened to the blood pounding through her ears saying: I am alone, I am alone, I am alone.

In the morning Susan lay in bed while he dressed.

He had been thinking things out in the night, because now he said: 'Susan, why don't we make a foursome?'

Of course, she said to herself, of course he would be bound to say that. If one is sensible, if one is reasonable, if one never allows oneself a base thought or an envious emotion, naturally one says: Let's make a foursome!

'Why not?' she said.

'We could all meet for lunch. I mean, it's ridiculous, you sneaking off to filthy hotels, and me staying late at the office, and all the lies everyone has to tell.'

What on earth did I say his name was? – she panicked, then said: 'I think it's a good idea, but Michael is away at the moment. When he comes back though – and I'm sure you two would like each other.'

'He's away, is he? – so that's why you've been . . .' Her husband put his hand to the knot of his tie in a gesture of male coquetry she would not before have associated with him; and he bent to kiss her cheek with the expression that goes with the words: Oh, you naughty little puss! And she felt its answering look, naughty and coy, come on to her face.

Inside she was dissolving in horror at them both, at how far they had both sunk from honesty of emotion.

So now she was saddled with a lover, and he had a mistress! How ordinary, how reassuring, how jolly! And now they would make a foursome of it, and go about to theatres and restaurants. After all, the Rawlingses could well afford that sort of thing, and presumably the publisher Michael Plant could afford to do himself and his mistress quite well. No there was nothing to stop the four of them developing the most intricate relationship of civilized tolerance, all enveloped in a charming afterglow of autumnal passion. Perhaps they would all go off on holidays together? She had known people who did. Or perhaps Matthew would draw the line there? Why should he, though, if he was capable of talking about 'foursomes' at all?

She lay in the empty bedroom, listening to the car drive off with Matthew in it, off to work. Then she heard the children clattering off to school to the accompaniment of Sophie's cheerfully ringing voice. She slid down into the hollow of the bed, for shelter against her own irrelevance. And she stretched out her hand to the hollow where her husband's body had lain, but found no comfort there: he was not her husband. She curled herself up in a small tight ball under the clothes: she could stay here all day, all week, indeed, all her life.

But in a few days she must produce Michael Plant, and – but how? She must presumably find some agreeable man prepared to impersonate a publisher called Michael Plant. And in return for which she would – what? Well, for one thing they would make love. The idea made her want to cry with sheer exhaustion. Oh no, she had finished with all that – the proof of it was that the words 'make love', or even imagining it, trying hard to revive no more than the pleasures of sensuality, let alone affection, or love, made her want to run away and hide from the sheer effort of the thing . . . Good Lord, why make love at all? Why make love with anyone? Or if you are going to make love, what does it matter who with? Why shouldn't she simply walk into the street, pick up a man and have a roaring sexual affair with him. Why not? Or even with 'Fred'? What difference did it make.

But she had let herself in for it – an interminable stretch of time with a lover, called Michael, as part of a gallant civilized foursome. Well she could not, and she would not.

She got up, dressed, went down to find Mrs Parkes, and asked her for the loan of a pound, since Matthew, she said, had forgotten to leave her money. She exchanged with Mrs Parkes variations on the theme that husbands are all the same, they don't think, and without saying a word to Sophie, whose voice could be heard upstairs from the telephone, walked to the Underground, travelled to South Kensington, changed to the Inner Circle, got out at Paddington, and walked to Fred's Hotel. There she told Fred that she wasn't going on holiday after all, she needed the room. She would have to wait an hour, Fred said. She went to a busy tearoom-cum-restaurant round the corner, and sat watching the people flow in and out the door that kept swinging open and shut, watched them mingle and merge and separate, felt her being flow into them, into their movement. When the hour was up she left a half-crown for her pot of tea, and left the place without looking back at it, just as she had left her house, the big, beautiful white house, without another look, but silently dedicating it to Sophie. She returned to Fred, received the key of No. 19, now free, and ascended the grimy stairs slowly, letting floor after floor fall away below her, keeping her eyes lifted, so that floor after floor descended jerkily to her level of vision, and fell away out of sight.

No. 19 was the same. She saw everything with an acute, narrow, checking glance: the cheap shine of the satin spread, which had been replaced carelessly after the two bodies had finished their convulsions under it, a trace of powder on the glass that topped the chest of drawers; an intense green shade in a fold of the curtain. She stood at the window, looking down, watching people pass and pass, and pass until her mind went dark from the constant movement. Then she sat in the wicker-chair, letting herself go slack. But she had to be careful, because she did not want, today, to be surprised by Fred's knock at five o'clock.

The demons were not here. They had gone forever, because she was buying her freedom from them. She was slipping already into the dark fructifying dream that seemed to caress her inwardly, like the movement of her blood . . . but she had to think about Matthew first. Should she write a letter for the coroner? But what should she say? She would like to leave him with the look on his face she had seen this morning – banal, admittedly, but at least confidently healthy. Well, that was impossible, one did not look like that with a wife dead from suicide. But how to leave him believing she was dying because of a man – because of the fascinating publisher Michael Plant? Oh, how ridiculous! How absurd! How humiliating! But she decided not to trouble about it, simply not to think about the living. If he wanted to believe she had a lover, he would believe it. And he *did* want to believe it. Even when he had found out that there was no publisher in London called Michael Plant, he would think: Oh, poor Susan, she was afraid to give me his real name.

And what did it matter whether he married Phil Hunt or Sophie? Though it ought to be Sophie, who was already the mother of those children . . . and what hypocrisy to sit here worrying about the children, when she was going to leave them because she had not got the energy to stay.

She had about four hours. She spent them delightfully, darkly, sweetly, letting herself slide gently, gently, to the edge of the river. Then, with hardly a break in her consciousness, she got up, pushed the thin rug against the door, made sure the windows were tight shut, put two shillings in the meter, and turned on the gas. For the first time since she had been in the room she lay on the hard bed that smelled stale, that smelled of sweat and sex.

She lay on her back on the green satin cover, but her legs were chilly. She got up, found a blanket folded in the bottom of the chest of drawers, and carefully covered her legs with it. She was quite content lying there, listening to the faint soft hiss of the gas that poured into the room, into her lungs, into her brain, as she drifted off into the dark river.

AN OLD WOMAN AND HER CAT

Her name was Hetty, and she was born with the twentieth century. She was seventy when she died of cold and malnutrition. She had been alone for a long time, since her husband had died of pneumonia in a bad winter soon after the Second World War. He had not been more than middle-aged. Her four children were now middle-aged, with grown children. Of these descendants one daughter sent her Christmas cards, but otherwise she did not exist for them. For they were all respectable people, with homes and good jobs and cars. And Hetty was not respectable. She had always been a bit strange, these people said, when mentioning her at all.

When Fred Pennefather, her husband, was alive, and the children just growing up, they all lived much too close and uncomfortable in a Council flat in that part of London which is like an estuary, with tides of people flooding in and out: they were not half a mile from the great stations of Euston, St Pancras and King's Cross. The blocks of flats were pioneers in that area, standing up grim, grey, hideous, among many acres of little houses and gardens, all soon to be demolished so that they could be replaced by more tall grey blocks. The Pennefathers were good tenants, paying their rent, keeping out of debt; he was a building worker, 'steady', and proud of it. There was no evidence then of Hetty's future dislocation from the normal, unless it was that she very often slipped down for an hour or so to the platforms where the locomotives drew in and ground out again. She liked the smell of it all, she said. She liked to see people moving about, 'coming and going from all those foreign places'. She meant Scotland, Ireland, the North of England. These visits into the din, the smoke, the massed swirling people, were for her a drug, like other people's drinking or gambling. Her husband teased her, calling her a gipsy. She was in fact part-gipsy, for her mother had been one, but had chosen to leave her people and marry a man who lived in a house. Fred Pennefather liked his wife for being different from the run of the women he knew, and had married her because of it; but her children were fearful that her gipsy blood might show itself in worse ways than haunting railway stations. She was a tall woman with a lot of glossy black hair, a skin that tanned easily, and dark strong eyes. She wore bright colours, and enjoyed quick tempers and sudden reconciliations. In her prime she attracted attention, was proud and handsome. All this made it inevitable that the people in those streets should refer to her as 'that gipsy woman'. When she heard them, she shouted back that she was none the worse for that.

After her husband died and the children married and left, the Council moved her to a small flat in the same building. She got a job selling food in a local store, but found it boring. There seem to be traditional occupations for middle-aged women living alone, the busy and responsible part of their lives being over. Drink. Gambling. Looking for another husband. A wistful affair or two. That's about it. Hetty went through a period of, as it were, testing out all these, like hobbies, but tired of them. While still earning her small wage as a saleswoman, she began a trade in buying and selling second-hand clothes. She did not have a shop of her own, but bought or begged clothes from householders, and sold these to stalls and the second-hand shops. She adored doing this. It was a passion. She gave up her respectable job and forgot all about her love of trains and travellers. Her room was always full of bright bits of cloth, a dress that had a pattern she fancied and did not want to sell, strips of beading, old furs, embroidery, lace. There were street traders among the people in the flats, but there was something in the way Hetty went about it that lost her friends. Neighbours of twenty or thirty years' standing said she had gone queer, and wished to know her no longer. But she did not mind. She was enjoying herself too much, particularly the moving about the streets with her old perambulator, in which she crammed what she was buying or selling. She liked the gossiping, the bargaining, the wheedling from householders. It was this last which – and she knew this quite well of course – the neighbours objected to. It was the thin edge of the wedge. It was begging. Decent people did not beg. She was no longer decent.

Lonely in her tiny flat, she was there as little as possible, always preferring the lively streets. But she had after all to spend some time in her room, and one day she saw a kitten lost and trembling in a dirty corner, and brought it home to the block of flats. She was on the fifth floor. While the kitten was growing into a large strong tom, he ranged about that conglomeration of staircases and lifts and many dozens of flats, as if the building were a town. Pets were not actively persecuted

152

by the authorities, only forbidden and then tolerated. Hetty's life from the coming of the cat became more sociable, for the beast was always making friends with somebody in the cliff that was the block of flats across the court, or not coming home for nights at a time so that she had to go and look for him and knock on doors and ask, or returning home kicked and limping, or bleeding after a fight with his kind. She made scenes with the kickers, or the owners of the enemy cats, exchanged cat lore with cat-lovers, was always having to bandage and nurse her poor Tibby. The cat was soon a scarred warrior with fleas, a torn ear, and a ragged look to him. He was a multicoloured cat and his eyes were small and yellow. He was a long way down the scale from the delicately coloured, elegantly shaped pedigree cats. But he was independent, and often caught himself pigeons when he could no longer stand the tinned cat food, or the bread and packet gravy Hetty fed him, and he purred and nestled when she grabbed him to her bosom at those times she suffered loneliness. This happened less and less. Once she had realized that her children were hoping that she would leave them alone because the old rag-trader was an embarrassment to them, she accepted it, and a bitterness that always had wild humour in it welled up only at times like Christmas. She sang or chanted to the cat: 'You nasty old beast, filthy old cat, nobody wants you, do they Tibby, no, you're just an alley tom, just an old stealing cat, hey Tibs, Tibs, Tibs.'

The building teemed with cats. There were even a couple of dogs. They all fought up and down the grey cement corridors. There were sometimes dog and cat messes which someone had to clear up, but which might be left for days and weeks as part of neighbourly wars and feuds. There were many complaints. Finally an official came from the Council to say that the ruling about keeping animals was going to be enforced. Hetty, like the others, would have to have her cat destroyed. This crisis coincided with a time of bad luck for her. She had had flu; had not been able to earn money; had found it hard to get out for her pension; had run into debt. She owed a lot of back rent, too. A television set she had hired and was not paying for attracted the visits of a television representative. The neighbours were gossiping that Hetty had 'gone savage'. This was because the cat had brought up the stairs and along the passageways a pigeon he had caught, shedding feathers and blood all the way; a woman coming in to complain found Hetty plucking the pigeon to stew it, as she had done with others, sharing the meal with Tibby.

'You're filthy,' she would say to him, setting the stew down to cool in his dish. 'Filthy old thing. Eating that dirty old pigeon. What do you think you are, a wild cat? Decent cats don't eat dirty birds. Only those old gipsies eat wild birds.'

One night she begged help from a neighbour who had a car, and put into the car herself, the television set, the cat, bundles of clothes, and the pram. She was driven across London to a room in a street that was a slum because it was waiting to be done up. The neighbour made a second trip to bring her bed and her mattress, which were tied to the roof of the car, a chest of drawers, an old trunk, saucepans. It was in this way that she left the street in which she had lived for thirty years, nearly half her life.

She set up house again in one room. She was frightened to go near 'them' to re-establish pension rights and her identity, because of the arrears of rent she had left behind, and because of the stolen television set. She started trading again, and the little room was soon spread, like the last, with a rainbow of colours and textures and lace and sequins. She cooked on a single gas ring and washed in the sink. There was no hot water unless it was boiled in saucepans. There were several old ladies and a family of five children in the house, which was condemned.

She was in the ground-floor back, with a window which opened on to a derelict garden, and her cat was happy in a hunting ground that was a mile around this house where his mistress was so splendidly living. A canal ran close by, and in the dirty city-water were islands which a cat could reach by leaping from moored boat to boat. On the islands were rats and birds. There were pavements full of fat London pigeons. The cat was a fine hunter. He soon had his place in the hierarchies of the local cat population and did not have to fight much to keep it. He was a strong male cat, and fathered many litters of kittens.

In that place Hetty and he lived five happy years. She was trading well, for there were rich people close by to shed what the poor needed to buy cheaply. She was not lonely for she made a quarrelling but satisfying friendship with a woman on the top floor, a widow like herself who did not see her children either. Hetty was sharp with the five children, complaining about their noise and mess, but she slipped them bits of money and sweets after telling their mother that 'she was a fool to put herself out for them, because they wouldn't appreciate it'. She was living well, even without her pension. She sold the television set and gave herself and her friend upstairs some day-trips to the coast, and bought a small radio. She never read books or magazines. The truth was that she could not write or read, or only so badly it was no pleasure to her. Her cat was all reward and no cost, for he fed himself, and continued to bring in pigeons for her to cook and eat, for which in return he claimed milk.

'Greedy Tibby, you greedy *thing*, don't think I don't know, oh yes I do, you'll get sick eating those old pigeons, I do keep telling you that, don't I?'

At last the street was being done up. No longer a uniform, long, disgraceful slum, houses were being bought by the middle-class people. While this meant more good warm clothes for trading – or begging, for she still could not resist the attraction of getting something for nothing by the use of her plaintive inventive tongue, her still flashing handsome eyes – Hetty knew, like her neighbours, that soon this house with its cargo of poor people would be bought for improvement.

In the week Hetty was seventy years old, came the notice that was the end of this little community. They had four weeks to find somewhere else to live.

Usually, the shortage of housing being what it is in London – and everywhere else in the world, of course – these people would have had to scatter, fending for themselves. But the fate of this particular street was attracting attention, because a municipal election was pending. Homelessness among the poor was finding a focus in this street which was a perfect symbol of the whole area, and indeed the whole city, half of it being fine, converted, tasteful houses, full of people who spent a lot of money, and half being dying houses tenanted by people like Hetty.

As a result of speeches by councillors and churchmen, local authorities found themselves unable to ignore the victims of this redevelopment. The people in the house Hetty was in were visited by a team consisting of an unemployment officer, a social worker and a rehousing officer. Hetty, a strong gaunt old woman wearing a scarlet wool suit she had found among her cast-offs that week, a black knitted tea-cosy on her head, and black buttoned Edwardian boots too big for her, so that she had to shuffle, invited them into her room. But although all were well used to the extremes of poverty, none wished to enter the place, but stood in the doorway and made her this offer: that she should be aided to get her pension – why had she not claimed it long ago? – and that she, together with the four other old ladies in the house should move to a Home run by the Council out in the northern suburbs. All these women were used to, and enjoyed, lively London, and while they had no alternative but to agree, they fell into a saddened and sullen state. Hetty agreed too. The last two winters had set her bones aching badly, and a cough was never far away. And while perhaps she was more of an urban soul even than the others, since she had walked up and down so many streets with her old perambulator loaded with rags and laces, and since she knew so intimately London's texture and taste, she minded least of all the idea of a new home 'among green fields'. There were, in fact, no fields near the promised Home, but for some reason all the old ladies had chosen to bring out this old song of a phrase, as if it belonged to their situation, that of old women not far off death. 'It will be nice to be near green fields again,' they said to each other over cups of tea.

The housing officer came to make final arrangements. Hetty Pennefather was to move with the others in two weeks' time. The young man, sitting on the very edge of the only chair in the crammed room, because it was greasy and he suspected it had fleas or worse in it, breathed as lightly as he could because of the appalling stink: there was a lavatory in the house, but it had been out of order for three days, and it was just the other side of a thin wall. The whole house smelled.

The young man, who knew only too well the extent of the misery due to lack of housing, who knew how many old people abandoned by their children did not get the offer to spend their days being looked after by the authorities, could not help feeling that this wreck of a human being could count herself lucky to get a place in his Home, even if it was – and he knew and deplored the fact – an institution in which the old were treated like naughty and dim-witted children until they had the good fortune to die.

But just as he was telling Hetty that a van would be coming to take her effects and those of the other four old ladies, and that she need not take anything more with her than her clothes 'and perhaps a few photographs', he saw what he had thought was a heap of multicoloured rags get up and put its ragged gingery-black paws on the old woman's skirt. Which today was cretonne curtain covered with pink and red roses that Hetty had pinned around her because she liked the pattern.

'You can't take that cat with you,' he said automatically. It was something he had to say often, and knowing what misery the statement caused, he usually softened it down. But he had been taken by surprise.

Tibby now looked like a mass of old wool that has been matting together in dust and rain. One eye was permanently half-closed, because a muscle had been ripped in a fight. One ear was vestigial. And down a flank was a hairless slope with a thick scar on it. A cat-hating man had treated Tibby as he treated all cats, to a pellet from his airgun. The resulting wound had taken two years to heal. And Tibby smelled.

No worse, however, than his mistress, who sat stiffly still, bright-eyed with suspicion, hostile, watching the well-brushed, tidy young man from the Council.

'How old is that beast?'

'Ten years, no, only eight years, he's a young cat about five years old,' said Hetty, desperate.

'It looks as if you'd do him a favour to put him out of his misery,' said the young man.

When the official left, Hetty had agreed to everything. She was the only one of the old women with a cat. The others had budgerigars or nothing. Budgies were allowed in the Home.

She made her plans, confided in the others, and when the van came for them and their clothes and photographs and budgies, she was not there, and they told lies for her. 'Oh, we don't know where she can have gone, dear,' the old woman repeated again and again to the indifferent van-driver. 'She was here last night, but she did say something about going to her daughter in Manchester.' And off they went to die in the Home.

Hetty knew that when houses have been emptied for redevelopment they may stay empty for months, even years. She intended to go on living in this one until the builders moved in.

It was a warm autumn. For the first time in her life she lived like her gipsy forbears, and did not go to bed in a room in a house like respectable people. She spent several nights, with Tibby, sitting crouched in a doorway of an empty house two doors from her own. She knew exactly when the police would come around, and where to hide herself in the bushes of the overgrown shrubby garden.

As she had expected, nothing happened in the house, and she moved back in. She smashed a back window-pane so that Tibby could move in and out without her having to unlock the front door for him, and without leaving a window suspiciously open. She moved to the top back room and left it every morning early, to spend the day in the streets with her pram and her rags. At night she kept a candle glimmering low down on the floor. The lavatory was still out of order, so she used a pail on the first floor instead, and secretly emptied it at night into the canal which in the day was full of pleasure boats and people fishing.

Tibby brought her several pigeons during that time.

'Oh, you are a clever puss, Tibby, Tibby! Oh, you're clever, you are. You know how things are, don't you, you know how to get around and about.'

The weather turned very cold; Christmas came and went. Hetty's cough came back, and she spent most of her time under piles of blankets and old clothes, dozing. At night she watched the shadows of the candle flame on floor and ceiling – the window-frames fitted badly, and there was a draught. Twice tramps spent the night in the bottom of the house and she heard them being moved on by the police. She had to go down to make sure the police had not blocked up the broken window the cat used, but they had not. A blackbird had flown in and had battered itself to death trying to get out. She plucked it, and roasted it over a fire made with bits of floorboard in a baking-pan: the gas of course had been cut off. She had never eaten very much, and was not frightened that some dry bread and a bit of cheese was all that she had eaten during her sojourn under the heap of clothes. She was cold, but did not think about that much. Outside there was slushy brown snow everywhere. She went back to her nest, thinking that soon the cold spell would be over and she could get back to her trading. Tibby sometimes got into the pile with her, and she clutched the warmth of him to her. 'Oh, you clever cat, you clever old thing, looking after yourself, aren't you? That's right, my ducky, that's right, my lovely.'

And then, just as she was moving about again, with snow gone off the ground for a time but winter only just begun, in January, she saw a builder's van draw up outside, a couple of men unloading their gear. They did not come into the house: they were to start work next day. By then Hetty, her cat, her pram piled with clothes and her two blankets, were gone. She also took a box of matches, a candle, an old saucepan and a fork and spoon, a tin-opener and a rat-trap. She had a horror of rats.

About two miles away, among the homes and gardens of amiable Hampstead, where live so many of the rich, the intelligent and the famous, stood three empty, very large houses. She had seen them on an occasion, a couple of years before, when she had taken a bus. This was a rare thing for her, because of the remarks and curious looks provoked by her mad clothes, and by her being able to appear at the same time such a tough battling old thing, and a naughty child. For the older she got, this disreputable tramp, the more there strengthened in her a quality of fierce, demanding childishness. It was all too much of a mixture; she was uncomfortable to have near.

She was afraid that 'they' might have rebuilt the houses, but there they still stood, too tumbledown and dangerous to be of much use to tramps, let alone the armies of London's homeless. There was no glass left anywhere. The flooring at ground level was mostly gone, leaving small platforms and juts of planking over basements full of water. The ceilings were crumbling. The roofs were going. The houses were like bombed buildings.

But in the cold dark of a late afternoon she pulled the pram up the broken stairs and moved cautiously around the frail boards of a second-floor room that had a great hole in it right down to the bottom of the house. Looking into it was like looking into a well. She held a candle to examine the state of the walls, here more or less whole, and saw that rain and wind blowing in from the window would leave one corner dry. Here she made her home. A sycamore tree screened the gaping window from the main road twenty yards away. Tibby, who was cramped after making the journey under the clothes piled in the pram, bounded down and out and vanished into neglected undergrowth to catch his supper. He returned fed and pleased, and seemed happy to stay clutched in her hard thin old arms. She had come to watch for his return after hunting trips, because the warm purring bundle of bones and fur did seem to allay, for a while, the permanent ache of cold in her bones.

Next day she sold her Edwardian boots for a few shillings – they were fashionable again – and bought a loaf and some bacon scraps. In a corner of the ruins well away from the one she had made her own, she pulled up some floorboards, built a fire, and toasted bread and the bacon scraps. Tibby had brought in a pigeon, and she roasted that, but not very efficiently. She was afraid of the fire catching and the whole mass going up in flames; she was afraid, too, of the smoke showing and attracting the police. She had to keep damping down the fire, and so the bird was bloody and unappetizing, and in the end Tibby got most of it. She felt confused, and discouraged, but thought it was because of the long stretch of winter still ahead of her before spring could come. In fact, she was ill. She made a couple of attempts to trade and earn money to feed herself before she acknowledged she was ill. She knew she was not yet dangerously ill, for she had been that in her life, and would have been able to recognize the cold listless indifference of a real last-ditch illness. But all her bones ached, and her head ached, and she coughed more than she ever had. Yet she still did not think of herself as suffering particularly from the cold, even in that sleety January weather. She had never, in all her life, lived in a properly heated place, had never known a really warm home, not even when she lived in the Council flats. Those flats had electric fires, and the family had never used them, for the sake of economy, except in very bad spells of cold. They piled clothes on to themselves, or went to bed early. But she did know that to keep herself from dying now she could not treat the cold with her usual indifference. She knew she must eat. In the comparatively dry corner of the windy room, away from the gaping window through which snow and sleet were drifting, she made another nest – her last. She had found a piece of polythene sheeting in the rubble, and she laid that down first, so that the damp would not strike up. Then she spread her two blankets over that. Over them were heaped the mass of old clothes. She wished she had another piece of polythene to put on top, but she used sheets of newspaper instead. She heaved herself into the

163

middle of this, with a loaf of bread near to her hand. She dozed, and waited, and nibbled bits of bread, and watched the snow drifting softly in. Tibby sat close to the old blue face that poked out of the pile and put up a paw to touch it. He miaowed and was restless, and then went out into the frosty morning and brought in a pigeon. This the cat put, still struggling and fluttering a little, close to the old woman. But she was afraid to get out of the pile in which the heat was being made and kept with such difficulty. She really could not climb out long enough to pull up more splinters of plank from the floors, to make a fire, to pluck the pigeon, to roast it. She put out a cold hand to stroke the cat.

'Tibby, you old thing, you brought it for me, then, did you? You did, did you? Come here, come in here . . .' But he did not want to get in with her. He miaowed again, pushed the bird closer to her. It was now limp and dead.

'You have it, then. You eat it. I'm not hungry, thank you, Tibby.'

But the carcass did not interest him. He had eaten a pigeon before bringing this one up to Hetty. He fed himself well. In spite of his matted fur, and his scars and his half-closed yellow eye, he was a strong, healthy cat.

At about four the next morning there were steps and voices downstairs. Hetty shot out of the pile and crouched behind a fallen heap of plaster and beams, now covered with snow, at the end of the room near the window. She could see through the hole in the floorboards down to the first floor, which had collapsed entirely, and through it to the ground floor. She saw a man in a thick overcoat and muffler and leather gloves holding a strong torch to illuminate a thin bundle of

164

clothes lying on the floor. She saw that this bundle was
a sleeping man or woman. She was indignant – *her*
home was being trespassed upon. And she was afraid
because she had not been aware of this other tenant of
the ruin. Had he, or she, heard her talking to the cat?
And where was the cat? If he wasn't careful he would
be caught, and that would be the end of him! The man
with a torch went off and came back with a second
man. In the thick dark far below Hetty, was a small
cave of strong light, which was the torchlight. In this
space of light two men bent to lift the bundle, which
was the corpse of a man or a woman like Hetty. They
carried it out across the danger-traps of fallen and rotting boards that made gangplanks over the water-filled
basement. One man was holding the torch in the hand
that supported the dead person's feet, and the light
jogged and lurched over trees and grasses: the corpse
was being taken through the shrubberies to a car.

There are men in London who, between the hours
of two and five in the morning, when the real citizens
are asleep, who should not be disturbed by such
unpleasantness as the corpses of the poor, make the
rounds of all the empty, rotting houses they know
about, to collect the dead, and to warn the living that
they ought not to be there at all, inviting them to one
of the official Homes or lodgings for the homeless.

Hetty was too frightened to get back into her warm
heap. She sat with the blankets pulled around her, and
looked through gaps in the fabric of the house, making
out shapes and boundaries and holes and puddles and
mounds of rubble, as her eyes, like her cat's, became
accustomed to the dark.

She heard scuffling sounds and knew they were rats.
She had meant to set the trap, but the thought of her

165

friend Tibby, who might catch his paw, had stopped her. She sat up until the morning light came in grey and cold, after nine. Now she did know herself to be very ill and in danger, for she had lost all the warmth she had huddled into her bones under the rags. She shivered violently. She was shaking herself apart with shivering. In between spasms she drooped limp and exhausted. Through the ceiling above her – but it was not a ceiling, only a cobweb of slats and planks – she could see into a dark cave which had been a garret, and through the roof above that, the grey sky, teeming with incipient rain. The cat came back from where he had been hiding, and sat crouched on her knees, keeping her stomach warm, while she thought out her position. These were her last clear thoughts. She told herself that she would not last out until spring unless she allowed 'them' to find her, and take her to hospital. After that, she would be taken to a Home.

But what would happen to Tibby, her poor cat? She rubbed the old beast's scruffy head with the ball of her thumb and muttered: 'Tibby, Tibby, they won't get you, no, you'll be all right, yes, I'll look after you.'

Towards midday, the sun oozed yellow through miles of greasy grey cloud, and she staggered down the rotting stairs, to the shops. Even in those London streets, where the extraordinary has become usual, people turned to stare at a tall gaunt woman, with a white face that had flaming red patches on it, and blue compressed lips, and restless black eyes. She wore a tightly buttoned man's overcoat, torn brown woollen mittens, and an old fur hood. She pushed a pram loaded with old dresses and scraps of embroidery and torn jerseys and shoes, all stirred into a tight tangle, and she kept pushing this pram up against people as they stood in queues, or gossiped, or stared into windows, and she muttered: 'Give me your old clothes, darling, give me your old pretties, give Hetty something, poor Hetty's hungry.' A woman gave her a handful of small change, and Hetty bought a roll filled with tomato and lettuce. She did not dare go into a café, for even in her confused state she knew she would offend, and would probably be asked to leave. But she begged a cup of tea at a street stall, and when the hot sweet liquid flooded through her she felt she might survive the winter. She bought a carton of milk and pushed the pram back through the slushy snowy street to the ruins.

Tibby was not there. She urinated down through the hole in the boards, muttering, 'A nuisance, that old tea,' and wrapped herself in a blanket and waited for the dark to come.

Tibby came in later. He had blood on his foreleg. She had heard scuffling and she knew that he had fought a rat, or several, and had been bitten. She poured the milk into the tilted saucepan and Tibby drank it all.

She spent the night with the animal held against her chilly bosom. They did not sleep, but dozed off and on. Tibby would normally be hunting, the night was his time, but he had stayed with the old woman now for three nights.

Early next morning they again heard the corpse-removers among the rubble on the ground floor, and saw the beams of the torch moving on wet walls and collapsed beams. For a moment the torchlight was almost straight on Hetty, but no one came up: who could believe that a person could be desperate enough to climb those dangerous stairs, to trust those crumbling splintery floors, and in the middle of winter?

Hetty had now stopped thinking of herself as ill, of

the degrees of her illness, of her danger – of the impossibility of her surviving. She had cancelled out in her mind the presence of winter and its lethal weather, and it was as if spring were nearly here. She knew that if it had been spring when she had had to leave the other house, she and the cat could have lived here for months and months, quite safely and comfortably. Because it seemed to her an impossible and even a silly thing that her life, or, rather, her death, could depend on something so arbitrary as builders starting work on a house in January rather than in April, she could not believe it: the fact would not stay in her mind. The day before she had been quite clear-headed. But today her thoughts were cloudy, and she talked and laughed aloud. Once she scrambled up and rummaged in her rags for an old Christmas card she had got four years before from her good daughter! In a hard harsh angry grumbling voice she said to her four children that she needed a room of her own now that she was getting on. 'I've been a good mother to you,' she shouted to them before invisible witnesses – former neighbours, welfare workers, a doctor. 'I never let you want for anything, never! When you were little you always had the best of everything! You can ask anybody, go on, ask them then!'

She was restless and made such a noise that Tibby left her and bounded on to the pram and crouched watching her. He was limping, and his foreleg was rusty with blood. The rat had bitten deep. When the daylight came, he left Hetty in a kind of a sleep, and went down into the garden where he saw a pigeon feeding on the edge of the pavement. The cat pounced on the bird, dragged it into the bushes, and ate it all, without taking it up to his mistress. After he had finished eating, he stayed hidden, watching the passing people. He stared at them intently with his blazing yellow eye, as if he were thinking, or planning. He did not go into the old ruin and up the crumbling wet stars until late – it was as if he knew it was not worth while going at all.

He found Hetty, apparently asleep, wrapped loosely in a blanket, propped sitting in a corner. Her head had fallen on her chest, and her quantities of white hair had escaped from a scarlet woollen cap, and concealed a face that was flushed a deceptive pink – the flush of coma from cold. She was not yet dead, but she died that night. The rats came up the walls and along the planks and the cat fled down and away from them, limping still, into the bushes.

Hetty was not found for a couple of weeks. The weather changed to warm, and the man whose job it was to look for corpses was led up the dangerous stairs by the smell. There was something left of her, but not much.

As for the cat, he lingered for two or three days in the thick shrubberies, watching the passing people and, beyond them, the thundering traffic of the main road. Once a couple stopped to talk on the pavement, and the cat, seeing two pairs of legs, moved out and rubbed himself against one of the legs. A hand came down and he was stroked and patted for a little. Then the people went away.

The cat saw he would not find another home, and he moved off, nosing and feeling his way from one garden to another, through empty houses, finally into an old churchyard. This graveyard already had a couple of stray cats in it, and he joined them. It was the beginning of a community of stray cats going wild. They killed birds, and the field mice that lived among the grasses, and they drank from puddles. Before winter had ended the cats had had a hard time of it from thirst, during the two long spells when the ground froze and there was snow and no puddles and the birds were hard to catch because the cats were so easy to see against the clean white. But on the whole they managed quite well. One of the cats was a female, and soon there were a swarm of wild cats, as wild as if they did not live in the middle of a city surrounded by streets and houses. This was just one of half a dozen communities of wild cats living in that square mile of London.

Then an official came to trap the cats and take them away. Some of them escaped, hiding till it was safe to come back again. But Tibby was caught. Not only was he getting old and stiff – he still limped from the rat's bite – but he was friendly, and did not run away from the man, who had only to pick him up in his arms.

'You're an old soldier, aren't you?' said the man. 'A real tough one, a real old tramp.'

It is possible that the cat even thought that he might be finding another human friend and a home.

But it was not so. The haul of wild cats that week numbered hundreds, and while if Tibby had been younger a home might have been found for him, since he was amiable, and wished to be liked by the human race, he was really too old, and smelly and battered. So they gave him an injection and, as we say, 'put him to sleep'.

SPIES I HAVE KNOWN

I don't want you to imagine that I am drawing any sort of comparison between Salisbury, Rhodesia, of thirty years ago, a one-horse town then, if not now, and more august sites. God forbid. But it does no harm to lead into a weighty subject by way of the minuscule.

It was in the middle of the Second World War. A couple of dozen people ran a dozen or so organizations, of varying degrees of left-wingedness. The town, though a capital city, was still in that condition when 'everybody knows everybody else'. The white population was about ten thousand; the number of black people, then as now, only guessed at. There was a Central Post Office, a rather handsome building, and one of the mail sorters attended the meetings of the Left Club. It was he who explained to us the system of censorship operated by the Secret Police. All the incoming mail for the above dozen organizations was first put into a central box marked CENSOR and, was read, at their leisure, by certain trusted citizens. Of course all this was to be expected, and what we knew must be happening. But there were other proscribed organizations, like the Watchtower, a religious sect for some reason suspected by governments up and down Africa – perhaps because they prophesied the imminent end of the world? – and some fascist organizations, reasonably enough in a war against fascism. There were organizations of obscure aims, and perhaps five members and a capital of five pounds, and there were individuals whose mail had first to go through the process, so to speak, of decontamination, or defusing. It was this last list of a hundred or so people which was the most baffling. What did they have in common, these sinister ones whose opinions were such a threat to the budding Southern Rhodesian State, then still in the Lord Malvern phase of the Huggins/Lord Malvern/Welensky/Garfield Todd/Winston Field/Smith succession? After months, indeed years, of trying to understand what could unite them, we had simply to give up. Of course, half were on the Left, kaffir-lovers and so on, but what of the others? It was when a man wrote a letter to the *Rhodesia Herald* in solemn parody of Soviet official style – as heavy then as now – urging the immediate extermination by firing squad of our government, in favour of a team from the Labour Opposition, and we heard from our contact in the post office that his name was now on the Black List, that we began to suspect the truth.

Throughout the war, this convenient arrangement continued. Our Man in the Post Office – by then several men, but it doesn't sound so well – kept us informed of what and who was on the Black List. And if our mail was being held up longer than was considered reasonable, the censors being on holiday, or lazy, authority would be gently prodded to hurry things up a little.

This was my first experience of Espionage.

Next was when I knew someone who knew someone who had told him of how a certain Communist Party Secretary had been approached by the man whose occu-

172

pation it was to tap communist telephones – we are now in Europe. Of course, the machinery for tapping was much more primitive then. Probably by now they had dispensed with human intervention altogether, and a machine judges the degree of a suspicious person's disaffection by the tones of his voice. Then, and in that country, they simply played back records of conversation. This professional had been in the most intimate contact with communism and communists for years, becoming involved with shopping expeditions, husbands late from the office, love affairs, a divorce or so, children's excursions. He had been sucked into active revolutionary politics through the keyhole.

'I don't think you ought to let little Jackie go at all. He'll be in bed much too late, and you know how bad-tempered he gets when he is over-tired.'

'She said to me No, she said. That's final. If you want to do a thing like that, then you must do it yourself. You shouldn't expect other people to pull your chestnuts out of the fire, she said. If he was rude to you, then it's your place to tell him so.'

He got frustrated, like an intimate friend or lover with paralysis of the tongue. And there was another thing, he was listening to events, emotions, several hours old. Sometimes weeks old, as for instance when he went on leave and had to catch up with a month's dangerous material all in one exhausting twenty-four hours. He found that he was getting possessive about certain of his charges; resented his colleagues listening in to 'my suspects'. Once he had to wrestle with temptation because he longed to seek out a certain woman on the point of leaving her husband for another man. Owing to his advantageous position he knew the other man was not what she believed. He imagined how he would trail her to the café which he knew she frequented, sit near her, then lean over and ask: 'May I join you? I have something of importance to divulge.' He knew she would agree: he knew her character well. She was unconventional, perhaps not as responsible as she ought to be, careless for instance about the regularity of meals, but fundamentally, he was sure, a good girl with the potentiality of good wifehood. He would say to her: 'Don't do it, my dear! No, don't ask me how I know, I can't tell you that. But if you leave your husband for that man, you'll regret it!' He would press her hands in his, looking deeply into her eyes – he was sure they were brown, for her voice was definitely the voice of a brown-eyed blonde – and then stride for ever out of her life. Afterwards he could check on the success of his intervention through the tapes.

To cut short a process that took some years, he at last went secretly to a communist bookshop, bought some pamphlets, attended a meeting or two, and discovered that he would certainly become a Party member if it were not that his job, and a very well-paid one with good prospects, was to spy on the Communist Party. He felt in a false position. What to do? He turned up at the offices of the Communist Party, asked to see the Secretary, and confessed his dilemma. Roars of laughter from the Secretary.

These roars are absolutely obligatory in this convention, which insists on a great degree of sophisticated understanding between professionals, even if on opposing sides and even if at war – Party officials, government officials, top-ranking soldiers and the like – and the governed, ever a foolish, trusting, and sentimental lot.

First, then, the roar. Then a soupçon of whimsicality: alas for this badly ordered world where men so well equipped to be friends must be enemies. Finally, the hard offer.

Our friend the telephone-tapper was offered a retaining fee by the Communist Party, and their provisional trust, on condition that he stayed where he was, working for the other side. Of course, what else had he expected? Nor should he have felt insulted, for in such ways are the double agents born, those rare men at an altogether higher level than he could ever aspire to reach in the hierarchies of espionage. But his finer feelings had been hurt by the offer of money, and he refused. He went off and suffered for a week or so, deciding that he really did have to leave his job with the Secret Police – an accurate name for what he was working for, though of course the name it went under was much blander. He returned to the Secretary in order to ask for the second time to become just a rank-and-file Communist Party member. This time there was no roar of laughter, not even a chuckle, but the frank (and equally obligatory) I-am-concealing-nothing statement of the position. Which was that he surely must be able to see their view – the Communist Party's. With a toehold in the enemy camp (a delicate way of describing his salary and his way of life) he could be of real use. To stay where he was could be regarded as a real desire to serve the People's Cause. To leave altogether, becoming just honest John Smith, might satisfy his conscience (a subjective and conditioned organ, as he must surely know by now if he had read those pamphlets properly) but would leave behind him an image of the capricious, or even the unreliable. What had he planned to tell his employers? 'I am tired of tapping telephones, it offends me!' Or: 'I regard this as an immoral occupation!' – when he had done nothing else

175

for years? Come, come, he hadn't thought it out. He would certainly be under suspicion for ever more by his ex-employers. And of course he could not be so innocent, after so long spent in that atmosphere of vigilance and watchfulness, as not to expect the communists to keep watch on himself? No, his best course would be to stay exactly where he was, working even harder at tapping telephones. If not, then his frank advice (the Secretary's) could only be that he must become an ordinary citizen, as far from any sort of politics as possible, for his own sake, the sake of the Service he had left, and the sake of the Communist Party – which of *course* they believed he now found his spiritual home.

But the trouble was that he did want to join it. He wanted nothing more than to become part of the world of stern necessities he had followed for so long, but as it were from behind a one-way pane of glass. Integrity had disfranchised him. From now on he could not hope to serve humanity except through the use of the vote.

His life was empty. His resignation cut off his involvement, like turning off the television on a soap opera, with the deathless real-life dramas of the tapes.

He felt that he was useless. He considered suicide but thought better of it. Then having weathered a fairly routine and unremarkable nervous breakdown, became a contemplative monk – high Church of England.

Another spy I met at a cocktail party, in the course of chat about this or that (it was in London, in the late fifties), said that at the outbreak of the Second World War he had been in Greece, or perhaps it was Turkey, where at another cocktail party, over the canapés, an official from the British Embassy invited him to spy for his country.

'But I can't,' said this man. 'You must know that perfectly well.'

'But why ever not?' inquired the official; a Second Secretary I think he was.

'Because, as of course you must know, I am a Communist Party member.'

'Indeed? How interesting. But surely that is not going to stand in the way of your desire to serve your country?' said the official, trumping ferocious honesty with urbanity.

To cut this anecdote short – it comes from a pretty petty level in the affairs of men – this man went home, spent a sleepless night weighing his allegiances, and decided by morning that of course the Second Secretary was right. He would like to serve his country, which was engaged, after all, in a war against fascism. He explained his decision to his superiors in the Communist Party, who agreed with him, and to his wife and his comrades. Then, meeting the Second Secretary at another cocktail party, he informed him of the decision he had taken. He was invited to attach himself to a certain Army unit, in some capacity to do with the Ministry of Information. He was to await orders. In due course they came, and he discovered that it was his task to spy on the Navy, or rather, that portion of it operating near him. Our Navy, of course. He was always unable to work out the ideology of this. That a communist should not be set to spy on, let's say, Russia seemed to him fair and reasonable, but why was he deemed suitable material to spy on his own side? He found it all baffling, and indeed rather lowering. Then, at a cocktail party, he happened to meet a naval officer with whom he proceeded to get drunk, and they both suddenly understood on a hunch that they were engaged in spying on each other, one for the Navy, one for the Army. Both found this work without much uplift; they were simply not able to put their hearts into it, apart from the fact that they had been in the same class at prep school and had many other social ties. Not even the fact that they weren't being paid, since it was assumed by their superiors – quite correctly of course – that they would be happy to serve their countries for nothing, made them feel any better. They developed the habit of meeting regularly in a café where they drank wine and coffee and played chess in a vine-covered arbour overlooking a particularly fine bit of the Mediterranean where, without going through all the tedium of spying on each other, they gave each other relevant information. They were found out. Their excuse that they were fighting the war on the same side was deemed inadequate. They were both given the sack as spies, and transferred to less demanding work. But until D-Day and beyond, the British Army spied on the British Navy, and vice versa. They probably all still do.

The fact that human beings, given half a chance, start seeing each other's points of view seems to me the only ray of hope there is for humanity, but obviously this tendency must be one to cause anguish to seniors in the Diplomatic Corps, and the employers of your common or garden spy – not the high-level spies, but of that in a moment. Diplomats, until they have understood why, always complain that as soon as they understand a country and its language really well, hey presto, off they are whisked to another country. But diplomacy could not continue if the opposing factotums lost a proper sense of national hostility. Some Diplomatic Corps insist that their employees must visit only among each other, and never fraternize with the locals, obviously believing that understanding with others is inculcated by a sort of osmosis. And, of course, any diplomat who shows signs of going native, that is to say really enjoying the manners and morals of a place, must be withdrawn at once.

Not so the masters among the spies: one dedicated to his country's deepest interests must be worse than useless. The rarest spirits must be those able to entertain two or three allegiances at once; the counter-spies, the double and triple agents. Such people are not born. It can't be that they wake up one morning at the age of thirteen, crying: Eureka, I've got it, I was born to be a double agent! Nor can there be a training school for multiple spies, a kind of top class that promising pupils graduate towards. Yet that capacity which might retard a diplomat's career, or mean death to the small fry among spies, must be precisely the one watched out for by the Spymasters who watch and manipulate in the high levels of the world's thriving espionage systems. What probably happens is that a man drifts, even unwillingly, into serving his country as a spy – like my acquaintance of the cocktail party who then found himself spying on the Senior Service of his own side. Then, whether there through a deep sense of vocation or unwillingly, he must begin by making mistakes; is sometimes pleased with himself and sometimes not; goes through a phase of wondering whether he would not have done better to go into the Stock Exchange, or whatever his alternative was – and then suddenly there comes that moment, fatal to punier men but a sign of his own future greatness, when he is invaded by sympathy for the enemy. Long dwelling on what X is doing, likely to be doing, or thinking, or planning, makes X's thought as familiar and as likeable as his own. The points of view of the nation he spends all his time trying to undo, are comfortably at home in a mind once tuned only to those of his own dear Fatherland. He is thinking the thoughts of those he used to call enemies before he understands that he is already psychologically a double agent, and before he guesses that those men who must always be on the watch for such precious material have noticed, perhaps even prognosticated, his condition.

On those levels where the really great spies move, whose names we never hear, but whose existence we have to deduce, what fantastic feats of global understanding must be reached, what metaphysical heights of international brotherhood!

It is of course not possible to do more than take the humblest flights into speculation, while making do with those so frequent and highly publicized spy dramas, for some reason or other so very near to farce, that do leave obscurity for our attention.

It can't be possible that the high reaches of espionage can have anything in common with, for instance, this small happening.

A communist living in a small town in England, who had been openly and undramatically a communist for years, and for whom the state of being a communist had become rather like the practice of an undemanding religion – this man looked out of his window one fine summer afternoon to see standing in the street outside his house a car of such foreignness and such opulence that he was embarrassed, and at once began to work out what excuses he could use to his working-class neighbours whose cars, if any, would be dust in comparison. Out of this monster of a car came two large smiling Russians, carrying a teddy bear the size of a sofa, a bottle of vodka, a long and very heavy roll, which later turned out to be a vast carpet with a picture of the Kremlin on it, and a box of chocolates of British make that had a pretty lady and a pretty dog on it.

Every window in the street already had heads packed behind the curtains.

'Come in,' said he, 'but I don't think I have the pleasure of knowing who . . .'

The roll of carpet was propped in the hall, the three children were sent off to play with the teddy bear in the kitchen, and the box of chocolates was set aside for the lady of the house, who was out doing the week's shopping in the High Street. The vodka was opened at once.

It turned out that it was his wife they wanted: they were interested in him only as a go-between. They wished him to ask his wife, who was an employee of the Town Council, to get hold of the records of the Council's meetings, and to pass these records on to them. Now, this wasn't London, or even Edinburgh. It was a small, unimportant North of England town, in which it would be hard to imagine anything ever happening that could be of interest to anyone outside it, let alone the agents of a Foreign Power. But, said he, these records are open, anyone could go and get copies – you, for instance. 'Comrades, I shall be delighted to take you to the Town Hall myself.'

No, what they had been instructed to do was to ask his wife to procure them minutes and records, nothing less would do.

A long discussion ensued. It was all no use. The Russians could not be made to see that what they asked was unnecessary. Nor could they understand that to arrive in a small suburban street in a small English town

181

in a car the length of a battleship, was to draw the wrong sort of attention.

'But why is that?' they inquired. 'Representatives of the country where the workers hold power should use a good car. Of course, comrade! You have not thought it out from a class position!'

The climax came when, despairing of the effects of rational argument, they said: 'And, comrade, these presents – the bear, the carpet, the chocolates, the vodka – are only a small token in appreciation of your work for our common cause. Of course you will be properly recompensed.'

At which point he was swept by, indeed taken over entirely by, atavistic feelings he had no idea were in him at all. He stood up and pointed a finger shaking with rage at the door: 'How dare you imagine,' he shouted, 'that my wife and I would take money. If I were going to spy, I'd spy for the love of mankind, for duty, and for international socialism. Take those bloody things out of here – wait, I'll get that teddy bear from the kids. And you can take your bloody car out of here too.'

His wife, when she came back from the supermarket and heard the story, was even more insulted than he was.

But emotions like these are surely possible only at the lowest possible levels of spy material – in this case so low they didn't qualify for the first step, entrance into the brotherhood.

Full circle back to Our Man in the Post Office, or, rather, the first of three.

After sedulous attendance at a lot of left-wing meetings, semi-private and public – for above all Tom was a methodical man who, if engaged in a thing, always

182

gave it full value – he put his hand up one evening in the middle of a discussion about Agrarian Reform in Venezuela, and said: 'I must ask permission to ask a question.'

Everyone always laughed at him when he did this, put up his hand to ask permission to speak, or to leave, or to have opinions about something. Little did we realize that we were seeing here not just a surface mannerism, or habit, but his strongest characteristic.

It was late in the meeting, at that stage when the floor is well loaded with empty coffee cups, beer glasses and full ash trays. Some people had already left.

He wanted to know what he ought to do: 'I want to have the benefit of your expert advice.' As it happened he had already taken the decision he was asking about.

After some two years of a life not so much double – the word implies secrecy – as dual, his boss in the Central Post Office called him to ask how he was enjoying his life with the Left. Tom was as doggedly informative with him as he was with us, and said that we were interesting people, well-informed, and full of a high-class brand of idealism which he found inspiring.

'I always feel good after going to one of their meetings,' he reported he had said. 'It takes you right out of yourself and makes you think.'

His chief said that he, for his part, always enjoyed hearing about idealism and forward-looking thought, and invited Tom to turn in reports about our activities, our discussions, and most particularly our plans for the future, as well in advance as possible.

Tom told us that he said to his boss that he didn't like the idea of doing that sort of thing behind our backs because, 'say what you like about the Reds, they are very hospitable'.

183

The chief had said that it would be for the good of his country.

Tom came to us to say that he had told his boss that he had agreed, because he wanted to be of assistance to the National War Effort.

It was clear to everyone that having told us that he had agreed to spy on us, he would, since that was his nature, most certainly go back to his boss and tell him that he had told us that he had agreed to spy. After which he would come back to us to tell us that he had told his boss that . . . and so on. Indefinitely, if his boss didn't get tired of it. Tom could not see that his chief would shortly find him unsuitable material for espionage, and might even dismiss him from being a sorter in the post office altogether – a nuisance for us. After which he, the chief, would probably look for someone else to give him information.

It was Harry, one of the other two post office employees attending Left Club meetings, who suggested that it would probably be himself who would next be invited to spy on us, now that Tom had 'told'. Tom was upset when everybody began speculating about his probable supersession by Harry or even Dick. The way he saw it was that his complete frankness with both us and his chief was surely deserving of reward. He ought to be left in the job. God knows how he saw the future. Probably that both his boss and ourselves would continue to employ him. We would use him to find out how our letters were slowly moving through the toils of censorship, and to hurry them on, if possible; his chief would use him to spy on us. When I say employ, I don't want anyone to imagine this implies payment. Or, at least, certainly not from our side. Ideology had to be his spur, sincerity his reward.

It will by now have been noticed that our Tom was not as bright as he might have been. But he was a pleasant enough youth. He was rather good-looking too, about twenty-two. His physical characteristic was neatness. His clothes were always just so; he had a small alert dark moustache; he had glossy dark well-brushed hair. His rather small hands were well mani-cured – this last trait bound to be found offensive by good colonials, whose eye for such anti-masculine evi-dence (as they were bound to see it), then if not now, was acute. But he was a fairly recent immigrant, from just before the war, and had not yet absorbed the mores.

Tom, in spite of our humorous forecast that he would tell his boss that he had told us, and his stiff and wounded insistence that such a thing was impossible, found himself impelled to do just that. He reported back that his chief had 'lost his rag with him'.

But that was not the end. He was offered the job of learning how to censor letters. He had said to his boss that he felt in honour bound to tell us, and his boss said: 'Oh, for Christ's sake. Tell them anything you damned well like. You won't be choosing what is to be censored.'

As I said, this was an unsophisticated town in those days, and the condition of 'everybody knowing every-body else' was always leading to such warm human situations.

He accepted the offer because: 'My mother always told me that she wanted me to do well for myself, and I'll increase my rating into Schedule Three as soon as I start work on censoring, and that means an increment of fifty pounds a year.'

We congratulated him, and urged him to keep us

informed about how people were trained as censors, and he agreed to do this. Shortly after that the war ended, and all the camaraderie of wartime ended as the Cold War began. The ferment of Left activity ended too.

We saw Tom no more, but followed his progress, steady if slow, up the Civil Service. The last I heard he was heading a Department among whose duties is censorship. I imagine him, a man in his fifties, a husband and no doubt a father, looking down the avenues of lost time to those dizzy days when he was the member of a dangerous revolutionary organization. 'Yes,' he must often say, 'you can't tell me anything about them. They are idealistic, I can grant you so much, but they are dangerous. Dangerous and wrongheaded! I left them as soon as I understood what they really were.'

But of our three post office spies Harry was the one whose career, for a while at least, was the most rewarding for idealistic humanists.

He was a silent, desperately shy schoolboy who came to a public meeting and fell madly in love for a week or so with the speaker, a girl, giving her first public speech and as shy as he was. His father had died and his mother, as the psychiatrists and welfare workers would say, was 'inadequate'. That is to say, she was not good at being a widow, and was frail in health. What little energy she had went into earning enough money for herself and two younger sons to live on. She nagged at Harry for not having ambition, and for not studying for the examinations which would take him up the ladder into the next grade in the Post Office – and for wasting time with the Reds. He longed to be of use. For three years he devoted all his spare time to organization of the Left, putting up exhibitions, hiring halls and rooms, decorating ballrooms for fund-raising dances, getting advertisements for our socialist magazine – circulation two thousand, and laying it out and selling it. He argued principle with Town Councillors – 'But it's not *fair* not to let us have the hall, this is a democratic country, isn't it?' – and spent at least three nights a week discussing world affairs in smoke-filled rooms.

At the time we would have dismissed as beyond redemption anyone who suggested it, but I dare say now that the main function of those gatherings was social. Southern Rhodesia was never exactly a hospitable country for those interested in anything but sport and the sundowner, and the fifty or so people who came to the meetings, whether in the Forces, or refugees from Europe, or simply Rhodesians, were all souls in need of congenial company. And they were friendly occasions, those meetings, sometimes going on till dawn.

A girl none of us had seen before came to a public meeting. She saw Harry, a handsome, confident, loquacious, energetic, efficient young man. Everyone relied on him.

She fell in love, took him home, and her father, recognizing one of the world's born organizers, made him manager in his hardware shop.

Which leaves the third, Dick. Now there are some people who should not be allowed anywhere near meetings, debates, or similar intellect-fermenting agencies. He came to two meetings. Harry brought him, describing him as 'keen'. It was Harry who was keen. Dick sat on the floor on a cushion. Wild bohemian ways, these, for well-brought-up young whites. His forehead puckered like a puppy's while he tried to follow wild un-Rhodesian thought. He, like Tom, was a neat, well-set-up youth. Perhaps the Post Office, or at least in Rhodesia, is an institution that attracts the well-ordered? I remember he reminded me of a boiled sweet, bland sugar with a chemical tang. Or perhaps he was like a bulldog, all sleek latent ferocity, with its little bulging eyes, its little snarl. Like Tom, he was one for extracting exact information. 'I take it you people believe that human nature can be changed?'

At the second meeting he attended, he sat and listened as before. At the end he inquired whether we thought socialism was a good thing in this country where there was the white man's burden to consider.

He did not come to another meeting. Harry said that he had found us seditious and un-Rhodesian. Also insincere. We asked Harry to go and ask Dick why he thought we were insincere, and to come back and tell us. It turned out that Dick wanted to know why the Left Club did not take over the government of the country and run it, if we thought the place ill run. But we forgot Dick, particularly as Harry, at the zenith of his efficiency and general usefulness, was drifting off with his future wife to become a hardware-store manager. And by then Tom was lost to us.

Suddenly we heard that 'The Party for Democracy, Liberty and Freedom' was about to hold a preliminary mass meeting. One of us was delegated to go along and find out what was happening. This turned out to be me.

The public meeting was in a side room off a ballroom in one of the town's three hotels. It was furnished with a sideboard to hold the extra supplies of beer and sausage rolls and peanuts consumed so plentifully during the weekly dances, a palm in a pot so tall the top fronds were being pressed down by the ceiling, and a dozen stiff dining-room chairs ranged one by one along the walls. When I arrived, there were eleven men and women in the room, including Dick. Unable to understand immediately why this gathering struck me as so different from the ones in which I spent so much of my time, I then saw it was because there were elderly people present. Our gatherings loved only the young.

Dick was wearing his best suit in dark-grey flannel. It was a very hot evening. His face was scarlet with endeavour and covered with sweat, which he kept sweeping off his forehead with impatient fingers. He was reading an impassioned document, in tone rather like the Communist Manifesto, which began: 'Fellow Citizens of Rhodesia! Sincere Men and Women! This is the Time for Action! Arise and look about you and enter into your Inheritance! Put the forces of International Capital to flight!'

He was standing in front of one of the chairs, his well-brushed little head bent over his notes, which were hand-written and in places hard to read, so that these inflammatory sentiments were being stammered and stumbled out, while he kept correcting himself, wiping off sweat, and then stopping with an appealing circular glance around the room at the others. Towards him were lifted ten earnest faces, as if at a saviour or a Party Leader.

The programme of this nascent Party was simple. It was to 'take over by democratic means but as fast as possible' all the land and the industry of the country 'but to cause as little inconvenience as possible' and 'as soon as it was feasible' to institute a regime of true equality and fairness in 'this land of Cecil Rhodes'.

He was intoxicated by the emanations of admiration

189

from his audience. Burning, passionate faces like these (alas, and I saw how far we had lapsed from fervour) were no longer to be seen at our Left Club meetings, which long ago had sailed away on the agreeable tides of debate and intellectual speculation.

The faces belonged to a man of fifty or so, rather grey and beaten, who described himself as a teacher 'planning the total reform of the entire educational system'; a woman of middle age, a widow, badly dressed and smoking incessantly, who looked as if she had long since gone beyond what she was strong enough to bear from life; an old man with an angelic pink face fringed with white tufts who said he was named after Keir Hardie; three schoolboys, the son of the widow and his two friends; the woman attendant from the Ladies' cloakroom who had unlocked this room to set out the chairs and then had stayed out of interest, since it was her afternoon off; two aircraftmen from the RAF; Dick the convenor; and a beautiful young woman no one had ever seen before who, as soon as Dick had finished his manifesto, stood up to make a plea for vegetarianism. She was ruled out of order. 'We have to get power first, and then we'll simply do what the majority wants.' As for me, I was set apart from them by my lack of fervour, and by Dick's suspicion.

This was in the middle of the Second World War, whose aim it was to defeat the hordes of National Socialism. Communist Russia was twenty-five years old. It was more than a hundred and fifty years since the French Revolution, and even more than that since the American Revolution which overthrew the tyrannies of England. The Independence of India would shortly be celebrated. It was nearly twenty years after

190

the death of Lenin. Trotsky had only just been murdered.

One of the schoolboys, a friend of the widow's son, put up his hand to say timidly that he believed 'there might be books which we could read about socialism and that sort of thing'.

'Indeed there are,' said the namesake of Keir Hardie, nodding his white locks, 'but we needn't follow the writ that runs in other old countries when we have got a brand new one here.'

(It must be explained that the whites of Rhodesia, then as now, are always referring to 'this new country'.)

'As for books,' said Dick, eyeing me with all the scornful self-command he had acquired since leaving his cushion weeks before on the floor of our living-room, 'books don't seem to do some people any good, so why do we need them? It is all perfectly simple. It isn't right for a few people to own all the wealth of a country. It isn't fair. It should be shared out among everybody, equally, and then that would be a democracy.'

'Well, obviously,' said the beautiful girl.

'Ah yes,' sighed the poor tired woman, emphatically crushing out her cigarette and lighting a new one.

'Perhaps it would be better if I just moved that palm a little,' said the cloakroom attendant, 'it does seem to be a little in your way perhaps.'

'Never mind about the palm,' said Dick magnificently. 'It's not important.'

And this was the point at which someone asked: 'Excuse me, but where do the Natives come in?' (In those days, the black inhabitants of Rhodesia were referred to as the Natives.)

This was felt to be in extremely bad taste.

'I don't really think that is applicable,' said Dick

191

hotly. 'I simply don't see the point of bringing it up at all – unless it is to make trouble.'

'They do live here,' said one of the RAF.

'Well, I must withdraw altogether if there's any likelihood of us getting mixed up with kaffir trouble,' said the widow.

'You can be assured that there will be nothing of that,' said Dick, firmly in control, in the saddle, leader of all, after only half an hour of standing up in front of his mass meeting.

'I don't see that,' said the beautiful girl. 'I simply don't see that at all! We must have a policy for the Natives.'

Even twelve people in one small room, whether starting a mass Party or not, mean twelve different, defined, passionately held viewpoints. The meeting at last had to be postponed for a week to allow those who had not had a chance to air their views to have their say. I attended this second meeting. There were fifteen people present. The two RAF were not there, but there were six white trade unionists from the railways, who, hearing of the new Party, had come to get a resolution passed. 'In the opinion of this meeting, the Native is being advanced too fast towards civilization and in his own interests the pace should be slowed.'

This resolution was always being passed in those days, on every possible occasion. It probably still is.

But the nine from the week before were already able to form a solid block against this influx of alien thought – not as champions of the Natives, of course not, but because it was necessary to attend to first things first. 'We have to take over the country first, by democratic methods. That won't take long, because it is obvious our programme is only fair, and after that we can decide

192

what to do about the Natives.' The six railway workers then left, leaving the nine from last week, who proceeded to form their Party for Democracy, Liberty and Freedom. A steering committee of three was appointed to draft a constitution.

And that was the last anyone ever heard of it, except for one cyclostyled pamphlet which was called 'Capitalism is Unfair. Let's Join Together to Abolish it. This means You!'

The war was over. Intellectual ferments of this sort occurred no more. Employees of the post office, all once again good citizens properly employed in sport and similar endeavours, no longer told the citizens in what ways they were being censored and when.

Dick did not stay in the post office. That virus, politics, was in his veins for good. From being a spokesman for socialism for the whites, he became, as a result of gibes that he couldn't have a socialism that excluded most of the population, an exponent of the view that Natives must not be advanced too fast in their own interests, and from there he developed into a Town Councillor, and from there into a Member of Parliament. And that is what he still is, a gentleman of distinguished middle age, an indefatigable server on Parliamentary Committees and Commissions, particularly those to do with the Natives, on whom he is considered an authority.

An elderly bulldog of the bulldog breed he is, every inch of him.

THE STORY OF A
NON-MARRYING MAN

I met Johnny Blakeworthy at the end of his life. I was at the beginning of mine, about ten or twelve years old. This was in the early thirties, when the Slump had spread from America even to us, in the middle of Africa. The very first sign of the Slump was the increase in the number of people who lived by their wits, or as vagrants.

Our house was on a hill, the highest point of our farm. Through the farm went the only road, a dirt track, from the railway station seven miles away, our shopping and mail centre, to the farms farther on. Our nearest neighbours were three, four and seven miles away. We could see their roofs flash in the sunlight, or gleam in the moonlight across all those trees, ridges and valleys.

From the hill we could see the clouds of dust that marked the passage of cars or wagons along the tracks. We would say: 'That must be so-and-so going in to fetch his mail.' Or: 'Cyril said he had to get a spare part for his plough, his broke down, that must be him now.'

If the cloud of dust turned off the main road and moved up through the trees towards us, we had time to build up the fire and put on the kettle. At busy times for the farmers, this happened seldom. Even at slack times, there might be no more than three or four cars a week, and as many wagons. It was mostly a white man's road, for the Africans moving on foot used their own quicker, short-cutting paths. White men coming to the house on foot were rare, though less rare as the Slump set in. More often now, coming through the trees up the hill, we saw walking towards us a man with a bundle of blankets over his shoulder, a rifle swinging in his hand. In the blanket-roll was always a frying-pan and a can of water, sometimes a couple of tins of bully beef, or a Bible, matches, a twist of dried meat. Sometimes this man had an African servant walking with him. These men always called themselves Prospectors, for that was a respectable occupation. Many did prospect, and nearly always for gold.

One evening, as the sun was going down, up the track to our house came a tall stooped man in shabby khaki with a rifle and a bundle over one shoulder. We knew we had company for the night. The rules of hospitality were that no one coming to our homes in the bush could be refused; every man was fed, and asked to stay as long as he wanted.

Johnny Blakeworthy was burned by the suns of Africa to a dark brown, and his eyes in a dried wrinkled face were grey, the whites much inflamed by the glare. He kept screwing up his eyes, as if in sunlight, and then, in a remembered effort of will, letting loose his muscles, so that his face kept clenching and unclenching like a fist. He was thin: he spoke of having had malaria recently. He was old: it was not only the sun that had so deeply lined his face. In his blanket-roll he had, as well as the inevitable frying-pan, an enamel one-pint saucepan, a pound of tea, some dried milk, and a change of clothing. He wore long, heavy khaki trousers for protection against lashing grasses and grass-seeds, and a khaki bush-shirt. He also owned a washed-out grey sweater for frosty nights. Among these items was a corner of a sack full of maize meal. The presence of the maize flour was a statement, and probably unambiguous, for the Africans ate maize-meal porridge as their staple food. It was cheap, easily obtainable, quickly cooked, nourishing, but white men did not eat it, at least not as the basis of their diet, because they did not wish to be put on the same level as Africans. The fact that this man carried it was why my father, discussing him later with my mother, said: 'He's probably gone native.'

This was not a criticism. Or rather, while with one part of the collective ethos the white men might say, 'He's gone native!' – and in anger – with a different part of their minds, or at different times, it could be said in bitter envy. But that is another story . . .

Johnny Blakeworthy was of course asked to stay for supper and for the night. At the lamplit table, which was covered with every sort of food, he kept saying how good it was to see so much real food again, but it was in a vaguely polite way, as if he was having to remind himself that this was how he should feel. His plate was loaded with food, and he ate, but kept forgetting to eat, so that my mother had to remind him, putting a little bit more of nice undercut, a splash of gravy, helpings of carrots and spinach from the garden. But by the end he had eaten very little, and hadn't spoken much either, though the meal gave an impression of much conversation and interest and eating, like a feast, so great was our hunger for company, so many were our questions. Particularly the two children questioned and demanded, for the life of such a man, walking quietly by himself through the bush, sometimes twenty miles or more a day, sleeping by himself under the stars, or the moon, or whatever weather the seasons sent him, prospecting when he wished, stopping to rest when he needed – such a life, it goes without saying, set us restlessly dreaming of lives different from those we were set towards by school and by parents.

We did learn that he had been on the road for 'some time, yes, some time now, yes'. That he was sixty. That he had been born in England, in the south, near Canterbury. That he had been adventuring up and down and around southern Africa all his life – but adventure was not the word he used, it was the word we children repeated until we saw that it made him uncomfortable. He had mined: had indeed owned his own mine. Had farmed, but had not done well. Had done all kinds of work, but 'I like to be my own master.' He had owned a store, but 'I get restless, and I must be on the move.'

Now there was nothing in this we hadn't heard before – every time, indeed, that such a wanderer came to our door. There was nothing out of the ordinary in his extraordinariness. Except, perhaps, as we remembered later, sucking all the stimulation we could out of the visit, discussing it for days, he did not have a prospector's pan, nor had he asked my father for permission to prospect on this farm. We could not remember a prospector who had failed to become excited by the farm, for it was full of chipped rocks and reefs, trenches and shafts, which some people said went back to the Phoenicians. You couldn't walk a hundred yards without seeing signs ancient and modern of the search for gold. The district was called 'Blanket' because it had running through it reefs of the same formation as reefs called Banket on the Rand. The name alone was like a signpost.

But Johnny said he liked to be on his way by the time the sun was up.

I saw him leave, down the track that was sun-flushed, the trees all rosy on one side. He shambled away out of sight, a tall, much too thin, rather stooping man in washed-out khaki and soft hide shoes.

Some months later, another man out of work and occupying himself with prospecting, was asked if he had ever met up with Johnny Blakeworthy, and he said yes, he had indeed! He went on with indignation to say that 'he had gone native' in the Valley. The indignation was false, and we assumed that this man too might have 'gone native', or that he wished he had, or could. But Johnny's lack of prospecting-pan, his maize meal, his look at the supper table of being out of place and unfamiliar – all was explained. 'Going native' implied that a man would have a 'bush wife', but it seemed Johnny did not.

'He said he's had enough of the womenfolk, he's gone to get out of their way,' said this visitor.

I did not describe, in its place, the thing about Johnny's visit that struck us most, because at the time it did not strike us as more than agreeably quaint. It was only much later that the letter he wrote us matched up with others, and made a pattern.

Three days after Johnny's visit to us, a letter arrived from him. I remember my father expected to find that it would ask, after all, for permission to prospect. But any sort of letter was odd. Letter-writing equipment did not form part of a tramp's gear. The letter was on blue Croxley writing-paper, and in a blue Croxley

198

envelope, and the writing was as neat as a child's. It was a 'bread-and-butter letter'. He said that he had very much enjoyed our kind hospitality, and the fine cooking of the lady of the house. He was grateful for the opportunity of making our acquaintance. 'With my best wishes, yours very truly, Johnny Blakeworthy.'

Once he had been a well-brought-up little boy from a small English country town. 'You must always write and say thank-you after enjoying hospitality, Johnny.'

We talked about the letter for a long time. He must have dropped in at the nearest store after leaving our farm to go north. It was twenty miles away. He probably bought a single sheet of paper and a lone envelope. This meant that he had got them from the African part of the store, where such small retailing went on – at vast profit, of course, to the storekeeper. He must have bought one stamp, and walked across to the post office to hand the letter over the counter. Then, due having been paid to his upbringing, he moved back to the African tribe where he lived – beyond post offices, letter-writing, and the other impedimenta that went with being a white man.

The next glimpse I had of the man, I still have no idea where to fit into the pattern I was at last able to make.

It was years later. I was a young woman at a morning tea-party. This one, like all others of its kind, was an excuse for gossip, and most of that was – of course, since we were young married women – about men and marriage. A girl, married not more than a year, much in love, and unwilling to sacrifice her husband to the collective, talked instead about her aunt from the Orange Free State. 'She was married for years to a real bad one, and then up he got and walked out. All she heard from him was a nice letter, you know, like a letter after a party or something. It said, "Thank you very much for the nice time." Can you beat that? And later still she found she had never been married to him because all the time he was married to someone else.'

'Was she happy?' one of us asked, and the girl said, 'She was nuts all right, she said it was the best time of her life.'

'Then what was she complaining about?'

'What got her was, having to say Spinster, when she was as good as married all those years. And that letter got her goat, "I feel I must write and thank you for . . ." something like that.'

'What was his name?' I asked, suddenly understanding what was itching at the back of my mind.

'I don't remember. Johnny something-or-other.'

That was all that came out of that most typical of South African scenes, the morning tea-party on the deep shady veranda, the trays covered with every kind of cake and biscuit, the gossiping young women watching their offspring at play under the trees, filling in a morning of their lazy lives before going back to their respective homes where they would find their meals cooked for them, the tables laid, and their husbands waiting. That tea-party was thirty years ago, and still that town has not grown so wide that the men can't drive home to take their midday meals with their families. I am talking of white families, of course.

The next bit of the puzzle came in the shape of a story which I read in a local paper, of the kind that gets itself printed in the spare hours of presses responsible for much more renowned newspapers. This one was called the *Valley Advertiser*, and its circulation might have been ten thousand. The story was headed:

OUR PRIZE-WINNING STORY, 'THE FRAGRANT BLACK ALOE', BY OUR NEW DISCOVERY, ALAN McGINNERY.

When I have nothing better to do, I like to stroll down Main Street, to see the day's news being created, to catch fragments of talk, and to make up stories about what I hear. Most people enjoy coincidences, it gives them something to talk about. But when there are too many, it makes an unpleasant feeling that the long arm of coincidence is pointing to a region where a rational person is likely to feel uncomfortable. This morning was like that. It began in a flower shop. There a woman with a shopping list was saying to the salesman: 'Do you sell black aloes?' It sounded like something to eat.

'Never heard of them,' said he. 'But I have a fine range of succulents. I can sell you a miniature rock-garden on a tray.'

'No, no, no. I don't want the ordinary aloes. I've got all those. I want the Scented Black Aloe.'

Ten minutes later, waiting to buy a toothbrush at the cosmetic counter at our chemist, Harry's Farmacy, I heard a woman ask for a bottle of Black Aloe.

Hello, I thought, black aloes have suddenly come into my life!

'We don't stock anything like that,' said the sales-girl, offering rose, honeysuckle, lilac, white violets and jasmine, while obviously reflecting that black aloes must make a bitter kind of perfume.

Half an hour later I was in a seed shop, and when I heard a petulant female voice ask, 'Do you stock succulents?' then I knew what was coming. This had happened to me before, but I couldn't remember where or when. Never before had I heard of the

201

Scented Black Aloe, and here it was, three times in an hour.

When she had gone I asked the salesman, 'Tell me, is there such a thing as the Scented Black Aloe?'

'Your guess is as good as mine,' he said. 'But people always want what's difficult to find.'

And at that moment I remembered where I had heard that querulous, sad, insistent, hungry note in a voice before (voices, as it turned out!) – the note that means that the Scented Black Aloe represents, for that time, all the heart's desire.

It was before the war. I was in the Cape and I had to get to Nairobi. I had driven the route before, and I wanted to get it over. Every couple of hours or so you pass through some little dorp, and they are all the same. They are hot, and dusty. In the tea-room there is a crowd eating ice-cream and talking about motor cycles and film stars. In the bars men stand drinking beer. The restaurant, if there is one, is bad, or pretentious. The waitress longs only for the day when she can get to the big city, and she says the name of the city as if it was Paris, or London, but when you reach it, two hundred or five hundred miles on, it is a slightly larger dorp, with the same dusty trees, the same tea-room, the same bar, and five thousand people instead of a hundred.

On the evening of the third day I was in the northern Transvaal, and when I wanted to stop for the night, the sun was blood-red through a haze of dust, and the main street was full of cattle and people. There was the yearly Farmers' Show in progress, and the hotel was full. The proprietor said there was a woman who took in people in emergencies.

The house was by itself at the end of a straggling

dusty street, under a large jacaranda tree. It was small, with chocolate-coloured trellis-work along the veranda, and the roof was sagging under scarlet bougainvillaea. The woman who came to the door was a plump, dark-haired creature in a pink apron, her hands floury with cooking.

She said the room was not ready. I said that I had come all the way from Bloemfontein that morning, and she said, 'Come in, my second husband was from there when he came here in the beginning.'

Outside the house was all dust, and the glare was bad, but inside it was cosy, with flowers and ribbons and cushions and china behind glass. In every conceivable place were pictures of the same man. You couldn't get away from them. He smiled down from the bathroom wall, and if you opened a cupboard door, there he was, stuck up among the dishes.

She spent two hours cooking a meal, said over and over again how a woman has to spend all her day cooking a meal that is eaten in five minutes, inquired after my tastes in food, offered second helpings. In between, she talked about her husband. It seemed that four years ago a man had arrived in the week of the Show, asking for a bed. She never liked taking in single men, for she was a widow living alone, but she did like the look of him, and a week later they were married. For eleven months they lived in a dream of happiness. Then he walked out and she hadn't heard of him since, except for one letter, thanking her for all her kindness. That letter was like a slap in the face, she said. You don't thank a wife for being kind, like a hostess, do you? Nor do you send her Christmas cards. But he had sent her one the Christmas after he left, and there it was, on the mantelpiece, With Best Wishes for a Happy Christmas. But he was so good to me, she said. He gave me every penny he ever earned, and I didn't need it, because my first hubby left me provided for. He got a job as a ganger on the railways. She could never look at another man after him. No woman who knew anything about life would. He had his faults of course, like everyone. He was restless and moody, but he loved her honestly, she could see that, and underneath it all, he was a family man.

That went on until the cocks began to crow and my face ached with yawning.

Next morning I continued my drive north, and that night, in Southern Rhodesia, I drove into a small town full of dust and people standing about in their best clothes among milling cattle. The hotel was full. It was Show time.

When I saw the house, I thought time had turned back twenty-four hours, for there were the creepers weighing down the roof, and the trellised veranda, and the red dust heaped all around it. The attractive woman who came to the door was fair-haired. Behind her, through the door, I saw a picture on the wall of the same handsome, blond young man with his hard grey eyes that had sun-marks raying out from around them into the sunburn. On the floor was playing a small child, obviously his.

I said where I had come from that morning, and she said wistfully that her hubby had come from there three years before. It was all just the same. Even the inside of the house was like the other, comfortable and frilly and full. But it needed a man's attention. All kinds of things needed attention. We had supper and she talked about her 'husband' – he had lasted until the birth of the baby and a few weeks beyond it – in the same impatient, yearning, bitter, urgent voice of her sister of the evening before. As I sat there listening, I had the ridiculous feeling that in hearing her out so sympathetically I was being disloyal to the other deserted 'wife' four hundred miles south. Of course he had his faults, she said. He drank too much sometimes, but men couldn't help being men. And sometimes he went into a daydream for weeks at a stretch and didn't hear what you said. But he was a good husband, for all that. He had got a job in the Sales Department of the Agricultural Machinery Store, and he had worked hard. When the little boy was born he was so pleased . . . and then he left. Yes, he did write once, he wrote a long letter saying he would never forget her 'affectionate kindness'. That letter really had upset her. It was a funny thing to say, wasn't it?

Long after midnight I went to sleep under such a large tinted picture of the man that it made me uncomfortable. It was like having someone watching you sleep.

Next evening, when I was about to drive out of Southern Rhodesia into Northern Rhodesia, I was half looking for a little town full of clouds of reddish dust, and crowding cattle, the small house, the waiting woman. There seemed no reason why this shouldn't go on all the way to Nairobi.

But it was not until the day after that, on the Copper Belt in Northern Rhodesia, that I came to a town full of cars and people. There was going to be a dance that evening. The big hotels were full. The lady whose house I was directed to was plump, red-haired, voluble. She said she loved putting people up for the night, though there was no need for her to do it since while her husband might have his faults (she said this with what seemed like hatred) he made good money at the garage where he was a mechanic. Before she was married, she had earned her living by letting rooms to travellers, which was how she had met her husband. She talked about him while we waited for him to come in to supper. 'He does this every night, every night of my life! You'd think it wasn't much to ask, to come in for meals at the right time, instead of letting everything spoil, but once he gets into the bar with the men, there is no getting him out.'

There wasn't a hint in her voice of what I had heard in the voices of the other two women. And I have often wondered since if in her case, too, absence would make the heart grow fonder. She sighed often and deeply, and said that when you were single you wanted to be married, and when you were married you wanted to be single, but what got her was, she had been married before, and she ought to have known better. Not that this one wasn't a big improvement on the last, whom she had divorced.

He didn't come in until the bar closed, after ten. He was not as good-looking as in his photographs, but that was because his overalls were stiff with grease, and there was oil on his face. She scolded him for being late, and for not having washed, but all he said was: 'Don't try to house-train me.' At the end of the meal she wondered aloud why she spent her life cooking and slaving for a man who didn't notice what he ate, and he said she shouldn't bother, because it was true, he didn't care what he ate. He nodded at me, and went out again. It was after midnight when he came back, with a star-dazed look, bringing a cold draught of night air into the hot lamplit room.

'So you've decided to come in?' she complained.

'I walked out into the veld a bit. The moon is strong enough to read by. There's rain on the wind.' He put his arm around her waist and smiled at her. She smiled back, her bitterness forgotten. The wanderer had come home.

I wrote to Alan McGinnery and asked him if there had been a model for his story. I told him why I wanted to know, told him of the old man who had walked up to our house through the bush, fifteen years before. There was no reason to think it was the same man, except for the one detail, the letters he wrote, like 'bread-and-butter' letters after a party or a visit.

I got this reply: 'I am indeed indebted to you for your interesting and informative letter. You are right in thinking my little story had its start in real life. But in most ways it is far from fact. I took liberties with the time of the story, moving it forward by years, no decades, and placing it in a more modern setting. For the time when Johnny Blakeworthy was loving and leaving so many young women – I'm afraid he was a very bad lot! – is now out of the memory of all but the elderly among us. Everything is so soft and easy now. "Civilization" so-called has overtaken us. But I was afraid if I put my "hero" into his real setting, it would seem so exotic to present-day readers that they would read my little tale for the sake of the background, finding that more interesting than my "hero".

'It was just after the Boer War. I had volunteered for it, as a young man does, for the excitement, not

207

knowing what sort of a war it really was. Afterwards I decided not to return to England. I thought I would try the mines, so I went to Johannesburg, and there I met my wife, Lena. She was the cook and housekeeper in a men's boarding-house, a rough job, in rough days. She had a child by Johnny, and believed herself to be married to him. So did I. When I made inquiries, I found she had never been married, the papers he had produced at the office were all false. This made things easy for us in the practical sense, but made them worse in some ways. For she was bitter and I am afraid never really got over the wrong done to her. But we married, and I became the child's father. She was the original of the second woman in my story. I describe her as home-loving, and dainty in her ways. Even when she was cooking for all those miners, and keeping herself and the boy on bad wages, living in a room not much larger than a dog's kennel, it was all so neat and pretty. That was what took my fancy first. I dare say it was what took Johnny's too, to begin with, at any rate.

'Much later – very much later, the child was almost grown, so it was after the Great War, I happened to hear someone speak of Johnny Blakeworthy. It was a woman who had been "married" to him. It never crossed our minds to think – Lena and me – that he had betrayed more than one woman. After careful thought, I decided never to tell her. But *I* had to know. By then I had done some careful field-work. The trail began, or at least began for me, in Cape Province, with a woman I had heard spoken of, and had then tracked down. She was the first woman in my story, a little plump pretty thing. At the time Johnny married her, she was the daughter of a Boer farmer, a rich one. I don't have to tell you that this marriage was unpopular.

It took place just before the Boer War, that nasty time was to come, but she was a brave girl to marry an Englishman, a *roinek*. Her parents were angry, but later they did the right thing and took her back when he left her. He did really marry her, in church, everything correct and legal. I believe that she was his first love. Later she divorced him. It was a terrible thing, a divorce for those simple people. Now things have changed so much, and people wouldn't believe how narrow and church-bound they were then. That divorce hurt her whole life. She did not marry again. It was not because she did not want to! She had fought with her parents, saying she must get a divorce, because she wanted to be married. But no one married her. In that old-fashioned rural community, in those days, she was a Scarlet Woman. A sad thing, for she was a really nice woman. What struck me was that she spoke of Johnny with no bitterness at all. Even twenty years later, she loved him.

'From her, I followed up other clues. With my own wife, I found four women in all. I made it three in my little story: life is always much more lavish with coincidence and drama than any fiction writer dares to be. The red-headed woman I described was a barmaid in a hotel. She hated Johnny. But there was little doubt in my mind what would happen if he walked in through that door.

'I told my wife that I had been big-game hunting. I did not want to stir up old unhappiness. After she died I wrote the story of the journey from one woman to another, all now of middle age, all of whom had been "married" to Johnny. But I had to alter the settings of the story. How fast everything has changed! I would have had to describe the Boer family on their farm, such simple and old-fashioned, good and bigoted people. And their eldest daughter – the "bad" one. There are no girls like that now, not even in convents. Where in the world now would you find girls brought up as strictly and as narrowly as those on those Boer farms, fifty years ago? and *still* she had the courage to marry her Englishman, that is the marvellous thing. Then I would have had to describe the mining camps of Johannesburg. Then the life of a woman married to a storekeeper in the bush. Her nearest neighbour was fifty miles away and they didn't have cars in those days. Finally, the early days of Bulawayo, when it was more like a shanty town than a city. No, it was Johnny that interested me, so I decided to make the story modern, and in that way the reader would not be distracted by what is past and gone.'

It was from an African friend who had known the village in which Johnny died that I heard of his last years. Johnny walked into the village, asked to see the Chief and, when the Chief assembled with the Elders, asked formally for permission to live in the village, as an African, not as a white man. All this was quite correct, and polite, but the Elders did not like it. This village was a long way from the centres of white power, up towards the Zambesi. The traditional life was still comparatively unchanged, unlike the tribes near the white cities, whose structure had been smashed for ever. The people of this tribe cherished their distance from the white man, and feared his influence. At least, the older ones did. While they had nothing against this white man as a man – on the contrary, he seemed more human than most – they did not want a white man in their life. But what could they do? Their traditions of hospitality were strong: strangers, visitors, travellers, must be sheltered and fed. And they were democratic: a man was as good as his behaviour; it was against their beliefs to throw a person out for a collective fault. And perhaps they were, too, a little curious. The white men these people had seen were the tax-collectors, the policemen, the Native Commissioners, all coldly official or arbitrary. This white man behaved like a suppliant, sitting quietly on the outskirts of the village, beyond the huts, under a tree, waiting for the Council to make up its mind. Finally they let him stay, on condition that he shared the life of the village in every way. This proviso they probably thought would soon get rid of him. But he lived there until he died, six years, with short trips away to remind himself, perhaps, of the strident life he had left. It was on such a trip that he had walked up to our house and stayed the night.

The Africans called him Angry Face. This name implied that it was only the face which was angry. It was because of his habit of screwing up and then letting loose his facial muscles. They also called him Man Without a Home, and The Man Who Has No Woman.

The women found him intriguing, in spite of his sixty years. They hung about his hut, gossiped about him, brought him presents. Several made offers, even young girls.

The Chief and his Elders conferred again, under the great tree in the centre of the village, and then called him to hear their verdict.

'You need a woman,' they said, and in spite of all his protests, made it a condition of his staying with them, for the sake of the tribe's harmony.

They chose for him a woman of middle age whose husband had died of the blackwater fever, and who had had no children. They said that a man of his age could not be expected to give the patience and attention that small children need. According to my friend, who as a small boy had heard much talk of this white man who had preferred their way of life to his own, Johnny and his new woman 'lived together in kindness'.

It was while I was writing this story that I remembered something else.

When I was at school in Salisbury there was a girl called Alicia Blakeworthy. She was fifteen, a 'big girl' to me. She lived with her mother on the fringe of the town. Her stepfather had left them. He had walked out.

Her mother had a small house, in a large garden, and she took in paying guests. One of these guests had been Johnny. He had been working as a game warden up towards the Zambesi river, and had had malaria badly. She nursed him. He married her and took a job as a counter-hand in the local grocery store. He was a bad husband to Mom, said Alicia. Terrible. Yes, he brought in money, it wasn't that. But he was a cold, hard-hearted man. He was no company for them. He would just sit and read, or listen to the radio, or walk around by himself all night. And he never appreciated what was done for him.

Oh, how we schoolgirls all hated this monster! What a heartless beast he was!

But the way *he* saw it, he had stayed for four long years in a suffocating town-house surrounded by a domesticated garden. He had worked from eight to four selling groceries to lazy women. When he came home, this money, the gold he had earned by his slavery, was spent on chocolates, magazines, dresses, hair-ribbons, for his townified stepdaughter. He was invited, three times a day, to sit down at a table crammed with roast beef and chickens and puddings and cakes and biscuits.

He used to try and share his philosophy of living.

'I used to feed myself for ten shillings a week!'

'But why? What for? What's the point?'

'Because I was free, that's the point! If you don't spend a lot of money, then you don't have to earn and you are free. Why do you have to spend money on all this rubbish? You can buy a piece of rolled brisket for three shillings, and you boil it with an onion and you can live off it for four days! You can live off mealie-meal well enough. I often did, in the bush.'

'Mealie-meal! I'm not going to eat native food!'

'Why not? What's wrong with it?'

'If you can't see why not, then I'm afraid I can't help you.'

Perhaps it was here, with Alicia's mother, that the idea of 'going native' had first come into his head.

'For crying out aloud, why cake all the time, why all these new dresses, why do you have to have new curtains, why do we have to have curtains at all, what's wrong with the sunlight? What's wrong with the starlight? Why do you want to shut them out? Why?'

That 'marriage' lasted four years, a fight all the way.

Then he drifted his way north, out of the white man's towns, and up into those parts that had not been 'opened up to white settlement', and where the Africans were still living, though not for long, in their traditional ways. And there at last he found a life that suited him, and a woman with whom he lived in kindness.